Cleo Edison Oliver

in Persuasion Power

SUNDEE T. FRAZIER

Illustrations by
Jennifer L. Meyer

Arthur A. Levine Books
An Imprint of Scholastic Inc.

Text copyright © 2017 by Sundee T. Frazier
Illustrations by Jennifer L. Meyer copyright © 2017
by Scholastic Inc.

This book is being published simultaneously in hardcover by Arthur A. Levine Books.

This book is a work of fiction. Names, characters, places, and incidents are either the product of the author's imagination or are used fictitiously, and any resemblance to actual persons, living or dead, business establishments, events, or locales is entirely coincidental.

Library of Congress Cataloging-in-Publication Data

Names: Frazier, Sundee Tucker, 1968– author.
Title: Cleo Edison Oliver in Persuasion power / Sundee T. Frazier.
Other titles: Persuasion power
Description: First edition. | New York, NY : Arthur A. Levine Books, an imprint of Scholastic Inc., 2017. | Summary: Successful businesswoman Fortune A. Davies has announced a new website where "kidpreneurs" can upload ads for their businesses and Cleo and her friend Caylee are sure this is the their big break to get funding for their personalized barrettes, Passion Clips—but producing an internet ad using their classmates is proving difficult, and Cleo is further distracted by her desire to find her birth parents.
Identifiers: LCCN 2016017797| ISBN 9780545822404 (pbk : alk. paper)
Subjects: LCSH: Adopted children—Juvenile fiction. | Birthparents—Juvenile fiction. | Internet advertising—Juvenile fiction. | Money-making projects for children—Juvenile fiction. | Racially mixed families—California—Juvenile fiction. | Best friends—Juvenile fiction. | CYAC: Adoption—Fiction. | Birthparents—Fiction. | Advertising—Fiction. | Business enterprises—Fiction. | Entrepreneurship—Fiction. | Family life—Fiction. | Best friends—Fiction. | Friendship—Fiction. | African Americans—Fiction.
Classification: LCC PZ7.F8715 Cj 2017 | DDC 813.6 [Fic] —dc23 LC record available at https://lccn.loc.gov/2016017797

10 9 8 7 6 5 4 3 2 1   17 18 19 20 21

Printed in the U.S.A.   40

First printing 2017

Book design by Mary Claire Cruz

To adoptees everywhere:
Your story matters.

Contents

1 ♦ The Next Fortune   5

2 ♦ Not-So-Lovely Language Arts   17

3 ♦ The Bug for Business   30

4 ♦ Unzipped   45

5 ♦ Persist and Prevail   57

6 ♦ Missing Pictures   64

7 ♦ The Lord Loves a Cheerful Buyer   78

8 ♦ Building the Buzz   94

9 ♦ Best. Idea. Ever!!!   108

10 ♦ Sounds like Trouble   117

11 ♦ Picture Day   131

12 ♦ Last-Minute Jitters   144

13 ◆ A Different Kind of Superpower   155

14 ◆ Pest Zoo   168

15 ◆ Ad Shoot — Take One   177

16 ◆ Friends Forever! ™   186

17 ◆ A Social Media Star Is Born   196

18 ◆ Meeting Mr. Banks   211

19 ◆ Persistence Pays   229

CLEOPATRA ENTERPRISES, INC.

818 Camphor Street

Altadena Heights, CA 91120

Fortune A. Davies, CEO
Fortune Enterprises, Inc.
150 Madison Avenue
New York, NY 10016

Dear Ms. Fortune A. Davies:

It has been almost a month since I last wrote, so I thought you might like an update. A lot has happened with Cleopatra Enterprises, Inc.—things that might sound not so good at first but that I am CONFIDENT will all work out for the best.

My last business, Cleo's Quick and Painless Tooth Removal Service, had several satisfied customers (see www.youtube.com /watch?v=8iQjyOZuMs for an example of one, my brother Josh). Some unfortunate decisions on my part forced us to have to close down (for now). <u>However</u>, I learned some very valuable lessons from this experience, which I passed on to my fifth-grade class as a part of my recent and most highly successful Passion Project presentation. One thing I learned is that I need to be more careful about how I use my POWERS of PERSUASION. I've got a lot of these powers, but according to my mom, there's a fine line between persuasion and being pushy. Sometimes I don't know my own strength.

The really good thing to come out of all this is that I have formed a board of directors: my parents, Charlie and Nicki Oliver, and my business partner's mom, Helyn Ortega. I am the CHAIRGIRL of the board, of course ☺. All future ideas will be run past the board <u>before</u> we start telling the whole world (something I failed to do last time).

My partner, Caylee, and I already have another business planned—CAYLEE'S CUTIES™. These aren't just any barrettes. They're personalized, and they're going to sell like snow cones on an Altadena Heights summer day (another one of my businesses).

Speaking of business, I need to get back to work. I've got a corporation to run. I just want you to know—<u>YOU ARE MY INSPIRATION!!!</u> And if you ever do a show on business kids, I hope you will think of me!!!

Your best admirer, who wants to be just like you,

Cleopatra Edison Oliver

Cleopatra Edison Oliver, CEO

P.S. I already have a poster of you on my wall, but I would LOVE, LOVE, LOVE to have a signed photograph. Thank you for sending me one if you can. Here is <u>my</u> last year's school photo from fourth grade. I have a dorky overbite and my bottom teeth are as crowded as the line outside your studio, but I will be getting braces soon so that I can have a perfect smile like you! ☺ ☺ ☺

◆ CHAPTER 1 ◆

The Next Fortune

C leo aimed the remote at the TV and punched in channel 24—the Good Life Network. *Fortune's network. Fortune's show would be on in less than ten minutes.*

Cleo had just settled into the cushy, faux-leather recliner when the doorbell rang.

"I'll get it!" Julian yelled. Her littlest brother tore through the house.

"I want to get it!" Josh shouted. The foot stomping doubled. There was a crash, the sound of piano keys being mashed, and Julian crying.

"What's going on down there?" Mom yelled from upstairs.

Cleo glanced at the large family photo hanging on the wall—her and her brothers' beaming brown faces, Mom's smiling white one, and Dad's sort-of tannish one. Why couldn't her brothers always be as still and quiet as they were in that picture?

Cleo headed for the front room when the doorbell rang again. She passed Josh and Jay wrestling on the wood floor. Barkley stood over them, barking. He trailed Cleo to the door, slowly. Their black lab still had a lot of pounds to shed.

"Hey, Jelly!" Cleo said, pushing Barkley back so she could open the door all the way.

Caylee carried her craft tote—a large, polka-dotted bag—over her shoulder. "Hi, Peanut Butter." Cleo and Caylee were like PB&J. They just went together.

"Ooo, a new Caylee's Cutie!" Cleo reached for the rainbow clip holding back one side of Caylee's chin-length, straight black hair. The word *Hope* was written in silver across the colorful arc.

"Our priest said rainbows are a promise that no matter how bad things seem, the world's not coming to an end."

Caylee peered around Cleo's shoulder at the boys. Josh was sitting on Jay's face. Jay flailed his fists but wasn't having much luck making contact. "Should we . . . do something?" she asked.

Josh rose up a little and farted. JayJay shrieked.

Brothers. Cleo shut the front door and motioned with her head for Caylee to follow. They slipped past Mom, who was putting the boys in separate corners—one in the living room and the other in the hallway near the bathroom. "Hi, Caylee!" Mom said from the hall.

"Hi, Miss Nicki!"

Cleo grabbed a box of Cheez-Its as they passed through the kitchen. They had just reached the family room when Mom called out, "You finished your homework, right, Cleo?"

Doughnuts and Disney!

She'd hoped Mom would be so distracted with Josh and Jay that she'd forget.

"Pretty much!" She and Caylee plopped onto the love seat. A lady on TV was dancing with a mop as if she were Cinderella with Prince Charming. A trail of sparkles followed her as the mop magically cleaned the kitchen floor.

Mom appeared in the doorway. Her short brown hair was disheveled. Her blue eyes locked with Cleo's brown ones. "Pretty much?"

"It'll be done before dinner." Cleo clasped her hands and looked at Mom with pleading eyes. *"Promise."*

"That's not our agreement, Cleo. It gets done before *Fortune.* Period."

Fortune's bouncy theme music came on. Cleo's pulse started to race. "But, Mom, it's starting!"

Mom held out her hand. Cleo resisted, watching out of the corner of her eye as Fortune entered the studio, hugging audience members and blowing kisses to the camera. "The remote, Cleo."

"It's not fair!" Cleo wailed. "Josh *never* has to do homework!"

Mom crossed her arms. "Really? You're going to compare yourself with a first-grader? You're in fifth grade, Cleo!"

Cleo's cheeks burned. Caylee's mom never stood over Caylee, demanding that she finish her homework. On the other hand, Caylee didn't need her mom to. Caylee kept all her assignments in a calendar on her iPad, with alarms to remind her when they were due.

Cleo handed over the remote with a huff and trudged out. They climbed the stairs to her room with its sign on the door: **Cleopatra Edison Oliver, CEO.** At the beginning of the school year, a few weeks before, Cleo had made the executive decision to change her middle name from Lenore to Edison (her grandparents' last name) in order to have the initials CEO, which also stood for chief executive officer, the person in charge of a company. She'd made the sign herself.

Cleo pushed on the door, feeling as flat as the soda she'd left sitting on her desk overnight.

"I can help you with your homework . . ." Caylee scanned the disaster zone. "If we can find it."

Even to Cleo's eyes, the room looked like a troll's cave. She'd really let it go since school had started. It was even worse than Josh and Jay's room, which was a verifiable rat's nest. Or more accurately, a mouse's. They'd found mouse poop in the closet not that long ago. The mouse was still at large.

"Seriously, where is it?" Caylee asked.

"Ummm . . ." Cleo put her finger to her mouth. "My room ate it?" They both laughed at that, and Cleo felt her enthusiasm returning. The carpeted floor was littered with clothes, magazines, and leftover flyers from her tooth-pulling business. Food scraps on a few dirty dishes. Beanie Babies, Barbies, and bubblegum wrappers. Dirty socks and underwear.

Cleo tossed things this way and that, until finally she found her backpack under the sweater she'd worn to school that day. She clambered onto her unmade bed and gave Beary—the floppy purple bear from her birth mom that she never slept without—a big squeeze. Caylee joined her and they got to work.

A few minutes later, Mom knocked on the door. She had to force her way in because of all the stuff on the floor. "Cleo." She sounded exasperated. "Your room!"

Uh-oh. Would Mom also make her clean her room before she could return to *Fortune*?

"How did it get so out of control?"

Cleo raised her shoulders and eyebrows at the same time. "Evil fairies?"

Mom took a deep breath. "You definitely need to clean this up before bedtime."

"But why? I'm the one who lives here." *Fortune and me*, she thought, glancing at the poster over her bed. Fortune stood with her arms outstretched. The gleam in her eye made it clear: She possessed the secret to living the best, most successful life ever. "It's where Fortune and I do all our best business brainstorming! And creative geniuses are always messy. Except Jelly." She mugged at her friend.

"That's great, but you can't let it get like this. Remember? We've got mice on the loose."

"I *know*, Mom."

"They're probably breeding a colony in here!"

Cleo shuddered. That image would help keep her on task—later. "Okay," she droned, admitting defeat.

"And don't forget, you're on bathrooms this week."

Ugh. Cleo *hated* cleaning bathrooms. Especially wiping the toilet seat. Her brothers had terrible aim. "Okay, *okay*." Every second Mom stood there nagging was another second Cleo wasn't watching *Fortune*.

At long last, she left them alone. They had Cleo's homework done in eighteen minutes and bounded back downstairs.

"Done already?" Mom asked.

"Done already! Caylee helped. But she didn't do it for me," she added quickly. She hoped her mom wouldn't want to check it. Who knew what great business knowledge she was missing every second she wasn't watching *Fortune*?

Mom gave them the go-ahead to watch TV and rushed into the living room where Josh and Jay ran and slid on the floor, yelling and making explosion sounds. For once, Cleo was glad her brothers were acting crazy. Barkley's barking filled the house.

"Outside, boys!" Mom called. "We can't afford another trip to the ER."

Cleo pulled on Caylee's arm. "Come on!" She hurried into the family room and clicked on the television. Three women sat in salon-style chairs in Fortune's studio. Cleo figured out quickly that they were "fempreneurs" (what Fortune called women business owners) who'd been invited onto the show for "power makeovers." Two women and a man—professional hairstylists—clipped and combed and flat-ironed the fempreneurs' hair into brand-new looks.

"I'm getting a hair makeover next week," Cleo said, flipping her braids over her shoulders. "In time for school pictures."

"Fun!" Caylee's brown eyes sparkled.

It *would* be fun, Cleo thought. She hadn't known if Mom would go for the idea, because of the expense. But Cleo had asked, Mom had said yes, and that's all Cleo needed. She imagined herself in a chair on Fortune's stage, getting her naturally coily-curly hair done in a sophisticated twist-n-curl just like Fortune's. Fabulous!

Only moments after they turned on the show, it was time for a commercial break. Cleo groaned and muted the sound. "I'm going to be on *Fortune* one day."

Caylee's face scrunched. "You think her show will still be on when we're that old?"

"Who said anything about being old?"

Caylee stared at her. "While you're still a kid?"

"Of course."

"Why would she have a kid on her show?"

"Kidpreneurs are the *future* of our country! And I've seen kids on her show already."

"Okay, but why would she have *you* on her show?"

"Why *wouldn't* she? I'll persuade her to have me on. Persuasion is my superpower, you know."

Caylee nodded emphatically. "I know."

"Plus, I'm the next Fortune A. Davies!"

Caylee sputtered and covered her mouth.

Cleo raised her chin, feeling a little hurt. "I could be!"

Caylee bumped into her playfully. "Hey, I brought you something." She pulled a large plastic container out of her tote bag. Inside was a sampling of her funky, handcrafted hair clips, each in its own compartment.

She plucked one out and handed it to Cleo—an old-fashioned lightbulb made of felt. The curvy metal part inside the bulb was done in glittery silver paint. It spelled Cleo's name!

"My own Caylee's Cutie!"

"Yep. Because you're always coming up with bright ideas. And now that your middle name is Edison, I especially thought a lightbulb would be perfect for you."

"Yes! As in Thomas—who is probably one of my great-great-great-great-great uncles or something."

"Exactly."

"Thanks, Jelly. I love it!" She gave Caylee a Bug-a-Hug (a hug so huge it made a person's eyes bug). "I'll show it off when we pitch our new business to our parents—I mean, our board of directors—tonight." Caylee's mom and older brother were coming for dinner so the girls could present their latest enterprise and hopefully get a thumbs-up to start promoting right away.

Fortune reappeared and Cleo scrambled for the remote.

"To all my sister-friends out there," Fortune was

saying, "we are so *over* the whole good hair–bad hair thing. Am I right?" The studio audience clapped and the camera did a close-up on two ladies nodding to each other. "And we all know we are *so* much more than our hair." More applause. "However . . . *however!* Your hair *is* an impression maker. So go ahead, girlfriends. Make an impression. Let your hair tell the world who you are!"

Something went *zing!* in Cleo's brain. *Tell the world who you are.* She grabbed Caylee's arm. "Fortune just gave us the perfect slogan for our barrette business."

"She did?"

"Yes. 'Tell the world who you are!' Because with our personalized hair clips, girls can let others know their hobbies and passions and what they're good at too. Like your artist palette clip and my lightbulb!"

"Hey, could we *call* them Passion Clips?" Caylee bit her bottom lip. "I've been feeling kind of weird about having a business with my name in it."

"Really?" Cleo couldn't imagine not wanting her name in the name of a business. In fact, her mom was in the process of test-marketing a new product Cleo had given her the idea *and* name for: Cleo's Canine Cookies™.

"Well . . . if you're sure . . ." Cleo tapped her finger on her lip. "It's perfect!" She held up her hand and Caylee slapped her a high five.

"Fortune will definitely have you on her show one day."

Cleo beamed. With Caylee's creative crafting and Cleo's Persuasion Power™, they'd be selling Passion Clips™ like crazy!

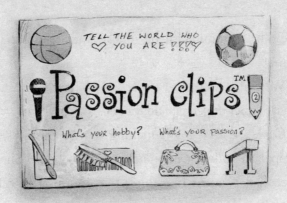

CHAPTER 2
Not-So-Lovely Language Arts

Mr. Boring (that really *was* his name, although he was actually the most interesting teacher Cleo'd ever had) blew into his duck call—*quack-quack-quack*! The class quieted down. Cleo thrust her arm in the air.

"Can it wait, Cleo? It's time for homework check."

"It can't, Mr. Boring."

"It can't, or *you* can't?" He crossed his long, skinny arms. Everything about Mr. Boring was long and skinny— his face, neck, body, legs, even feet.

"Both! I promise I'll be quick. And it's super-duper exciting!"

"Well, if it were just super, you'd have to wait. But since it's super-*duper*, whaddaya got?"

"Caylee and I are launching a new business, and Principal Yu said we can operate here at school!" She and Caylee had gone in first thing that morning to get his approval, at the insistence of their board of directors. By the time they'd left, they'd sold their first two pairs of clips—soccer balls and soccer cleats—for Principal Yu's daughter. He'd even promised to mention their business to the coach in case other girls on the team wanted to order from them.

"Definitely 'duper-worthy' news, Cleo. That's great. After lunch, I'll let you tell the class all about it. Consider it free advertising."

Cleo didn't want to wait until after lunch, but she didn't want to displease Mr. Boring more, so she agreed.

The school day had just started, which meant home-work check, where they were supposed to check their answers *quietly* and circle any they got wrong. Cleo looked at her paper—a page of completely confusing story problems that she'd rushed through before Caylee had come over to watch *Fortune*. She hadn't wanted to waste time asking Caylee to check them and miss even more of the show. Now she wished she had. They were *all* wrong. Ugh.

Cleo's desk was clustered with three desks belonging to her table buddies, Cole Lewis, Micah Mitchell, and Anusha Chatterjee. She leaned toward Cole. "Hey," she whispered. "Caylee and I are selling these *really* cool, personalized hair clips." She pointed to the lightbulb clipped into her braids. "Maybe you'd like to buy a pair for your sister?" Cole's twin was Lexie Lewis, who happened to be Cleo's archenemy number one, but hey, a sale was a sale.

"Which one?"

That stopped Cleo. She didn't know he and Lexie had another sister.

"Because if you mean Lexie, no way. She's got her own money."

"You have another sister?"

"Not technically. Neecie's our three-year-old cousin. But she lives with us. I'd buy one for her."

"Cleo, Cole. First warning." Mr. Boring wrote their names on the whiteboard. Cole gave Cleo a stink eye.

"I'd buy a pair," Micah whispered.

"Is there someone *you'd* be buying them for?" Cleo crooned.

Micah's eyes shifted back and forth. "Uh . . . no."

Cleo stared, nonplussed. "Shall I put you down for a pair, then?"

"Cleopatra Oliver," Mr. Boring said loudly, as though he'd possibly said it a few times already.

She looked at her teacher. "Yes, Mr. B?"

"How are you doing on checking those answers?"

"Why do we have to spend time figuring out things like how many passengers are on a train that doesn't even exist? I'm not planning on working for the railroad company."

Some of the other kids snickered.

"I know it's nowhere near as thrilling as the high-flying stakes of entrepreneurship, but you'll need to be able to do computations like this—*especially* in the world of business." He put a line on the board after her name. A strike! Cleo had *never* gotten a strike from Mr. B. Of course, it was only the end of September, but still, she'd hoped to go this whole year without getting one. *She* needed a "power makeover"—from "disruptive talker" (last year's report card comment) to productive, professional CEO. For the rest of homework check, her lips were zipped.

Finally, Mr. B gathered their papers. "Okay. Time to move on to lovely language arts! So, yesterday, we read poems and talked about metaphors. Quick, who can tell me what a metaphor is?"

Cleo thrust her arm in the air again.

"Cleo."

"Um . . . hmmm. It had something to do with hope and feathers. And you told us failure didn't really smell but it could have a stench, which I totally get. Failure *stinks*. Oh! And time is money! I definitely remember that one."

Mr. Boring nodded. "Okay . . . that's a start. You remember some of the metaphors we talked about, but what *is* a metaphor? Amelie?"

"I think it's when you compare one thing to something else and it makes your description more memorable by creating an image?"

Mr. B put his finger on his long, skinny nose. "Bingo!"

Cleo felt a jealousy attack coming on.

Amelie Martinet smiled. She flipped her long auburn hair over her shoulder. Everyone always said what cute dimples Amelie had. Cleo wished *she* had dimples instead of crowded front teeth and an overbite that needed braces to fix.

"This morning," Mr. B went on, "we're going to get started on writing our own poetry."

A few kids groaned, including Cleo.

"Don't worry. It's going to be fun. First, I want you to think about your personality."

Great! Cleo could definitely do that.

"For example, let's say you're cheerful, or chummy, or *chatty* . . ." He looked pointedly at Cleo. She gave him a sheepish grin. There were worse things a person could be.

"Or chill," Cole Lewis said, trying to sound cool.

Cleo rolled her eyes. *Or cheesy,* she thought.

"Exactly!" Mr. B said. "But your adjective doesn't have to start with *c-h*. Pick a word that describes you really well. Then I want you to come up with at least *five* similes— remember that's a metaphor that uses *like* or *as*—to illustrate that part of your personality. For example, I'm as crazy as a blizzard in July. I'm as crazy as a circus clown. I'm as crazy as a duck wearing a dress." People laughed. The image of a duck in a dress was pretty funny. The image of tall, skinny Mr. Boring in a dress was even funnier. "Got it?"

Cleo got it. She opened her language arts notebook. She would show Mr. B she could be focused. As focused as a telescope.

What adjective described her best? Definitely not focused. She could be crazy . . . but she didn't want to copy. She was friendly . . . but Caylee was friendlier. She was messy . . . hmmm, not exactly the trait she wanted to highlight with her teacher.

Cleo looked over to Anusha's paper. Upside-down reading was one of the most useful skills she'd gained from school.

I'm as quiet as a star in the nighttime sky, she had written. Wow. That was practically a poem already. And it was true—Anusha was the quietest girl in their class, maybe even in the whole school.

She read Micah's. *I'm as hungry as a bear that's just woken up from hypernation.*

"Being hungry isn't a part of your personality," she whispered.

Cole butted in. "I like it, man. I'm always hungry."

"And it's hi*ber*nation," Cleo pointed out.

"I like *hypernation* better," Micah said.

Micah *was* hyper, all right.

Cole pushed his notebook into her space and pointed to his paper. He smiled broadly. *I'm as chill as a Wendy's Frosty. I'm as chill as an ice cube on a frozen lake. I'm as chill as snow on a dead person.*

Cleo scrunched her face. *Snow on a dead person?* Ew.

"Hey, you need some help?" He raised an eyebrow at her blank paper. "I'm good at this stuff."

"No thanks."

She tapped her pencil eraser on the desk. Mr. Boring had called her enterprising more than once. She started to write: *I'm as enterprising as . . .*

Nope. Too hard. Language arts were *not* lovely. Not lovely at all.

Cole nudged her arm.

She was about to get as mad as a stepped-on snake.

"My sister landed a job because of you."

Huh? What was Cole Lewis talking about now?

She peered over her shoulder. Mr. Boring was on the other side of the room, helping Max-as-funny-as-a-whoopee-cushion-Peacock.

"What are you talking about?"

"The ad producers loved her missing teeth."

"Teeth? I only knocked out one," Cleo whispered. The knocked-out tooth had been unintentional. The punch, not so much. Lexie Lewis had made fun of her for being adopted. Worse than that. She'd said it was Cleo's freakishness that had caused her birth mom not to want her—that it was Cleo's fault she'd been given away. And Cleo just couldn't let the girl get away with saying that—about her or her birth mom.

"She lost another one before the audition. They said the spaces made her look"—Cole's eyelids fluttered— *"adorable."*

Cleo clapped her hand over her mouth, but some giggles escaped anyway.

French fries and Frito-Lay. Mr. Boring was headed their way. And she hadn't written a single word.

Persistent. Dad had called her Miss Persistent the night before, when they'd been talking about where they might advertise their Passion Clips if Principal Yu said no to doing it at school.

Persistent. That pretty much summed her up.

She crossed the last *t* just as Mr. Boring's hand landed on her shoulder.

"How's it going over here?"

Cleo looked up. "I think I might need to sit at the Thinking Desk to finish." The Thinking Desk was the place Mr. Boring put kids who were having a hard time getting their work done. Cleo figured it would be better to volunteer than to get sent there.

"Good choice, Cleo." Mr. Boring patted her back. "That's a sign of real maturity."

She took her notebook and went, being sure not to look at anyone along the way. She sat at the desk, determined to be *persistent* and finish her assignment.

But all she could think about at the Thinking Desk was her and Caylee's new business. How would they get the word out about Passion Clips at New Heights Elementary?

She snuck a piece of white paper from the shelving unit near the Thinking Desk and wrote **Passion Clips**™ across the top in big curlicue letters. Tell the world who you are!!! she added below that. She was into it now. "What's your hobby? What's your passion? Tell us what you like to do and we'll design hair clips just for you! One-of-a-kind barrettes for one-of-a-kind you. Handmade by Caylee Ortega and Cleo Oliver. $4 each or $7 a pair."

She added some drawings of possible barrettes: a microphone (she was thinking of Amelie, who loved to sing), a brush and comb (Mia Jeffers was a pro with hairstyling), a pencil (for anyone who liked to write—that *wouldn't* be Cleo), and a chef's hat and large stirring spoon, because they were things she could draw.

For the sporty girls, she drew a basketball (her personal favorite), soccer ball, and balance beam (for Steffy Lee, her friend the gymnast). She would have drawn a horse for Tessa Hutchfield, but she wasn't *that* good at drawing.

What would Lexie Lewis put in her hair to tell the world who *she* was? A mirror would be good for her—since she loved herself so much. Or a Trudy Ferretti purse, the kind she carried around school and made sure everyone knew was *not* a knockoff. Maybe a television. Whatever else Lexie Lewis was, she was determined to become a star.

She decided on the purse and was just putting on the finishing touches when Mr. Boring walked up. "You've moved on to something else, I see. All done with your similes, then?"

Cleo got as hot as something in an oven. "Not exactly, Mr. B . . ."

Mr. Boring squatted so his eyes were level with hers. "Cleo," he said seriously. "It seems like you're having an especially hard time staying focused today. What do you think we could do to keep you on track better?"

Cleo dropped her chin. "I'm sorry, Mr. Boring. It's just that I get kind of . . . kind of, well, *bored* when I have to do assignments that I don't really see the point of."

He pointed to the words on her ad. "What do you call this?"

"Ad copy."

He underlined Tell the world who you are!!! with his finger. "No, *this*."

"Oh, that's our business slogan."

"And a metaphor."

Her eyebrows pulled together. "It is?"

"Will your clips literally tell the whole world who the wearers are?"

"No, I guess not."

"So it's a metaphor. Will it help you sell your product?"

"I hope so!"

"Fantastic. So can we agree metaphors can be useful?"

She nodded.

"Good. You'll have to finish your simile assignment at home. Bring it back tomorrow."

"Okay."

He spoke to the class. "Who wants to share a simile?"

Micah was the first one to raise his hand. "I'm as hungry as someone who would eat the north end of a southbound duck."

At first, everyone was quiet. Then Rowdy Jimmy Ryerson blurted, "That's the duck's butt!" and the class erupted with "Ewwww!" and "Duck butt! Ha-ha-ha!" until Mr. Boring had to use his duck call to restore order. But, of course, the duck quacker just made everyone crack up more, given what they were laughing about.

Even Mr. Boring was laughing. "Well, Micah, you certainly have created a memorable image."

Micah may have been a bit different, but different could be good when it came to the world of business. Micah Mitchell was outside the box. Cleo just might have to recruit him to come and work for her.

CHAPTER 3

The Bug for Business

During first recess, Cleo took her ad to the office hoping to get it copied. She asked for Principal Yu, but he was not as helpful as she had hoped. He said something about not being able to fund students' personal activities with taxpayer money and sent her outside.

She didn't have an ad, but she had something better: her mouth. And Caylee's awesome samples. Outside, they focused on the sixth-graders and got four orders: two artist palette–paint brush sets, a pair of basketballs, and Yodas for LaLa Lopez, who everyone knew was a *Star Wars* fanatic.

At their class's lunch table, they got four more orders: horses and Tootsie Rolls for Tessa, microphones for Amelie, and pink balance beams for Steffy. Caylee wrote down exactly what each person wanted—including colors, whether they wanted their names on the clips, and any other important details.

On the playground after lunch, Cleo spotted a group of girls from Ms. Sanchez's fifth-grade class sitting and standing around the picnic table in the courtyard area.

Perfect. She hadn't had a chance to tell any of them about their new business and here a bunch of them were in one group.

She nudged Caylee and headed for the table, until one of the girls moved and she saw who was at the center. Lexie Lewis, of course.

Cleo drew a big breath and charged ahead. She couldn't avoid Lexie forever. She and Caylee stepped up to the circle just as Lexie exclaimed, "Can you believe I'm going to be the new face of Sunshine Sparkle flute-fravored beverage? They said I was adorable!"

Cleo laughed at Lexie's accidental switch of letter sounds.

"And why is that so funny?" Lexie scowled.

Cleo startled. "Oh. You said flute-fravored." She looked around the circle. A couple of girls giggled, but no one backed her up, and Lexie didn't admit to her mistake.

"Well, I wouldn't laugh if I were you. You could have cost me this job, going all kung fu on my face."

Cleo wanted so badly to say that it was Lexie's missing teeth—including one that Cleo had helped remove—that they'd really thought was adorable. But if the queen bee got angry, the other bees might scatter, or rally around in her defense, and Cleo couldn't waste this perfect promotional opportunity.

"That's really great about the ad, Lexie," she said.

Mia spoke, her face aglow. "It's going to air across the *whole country.*"

Somehow, in less than a year at New Heights Elementary, Lexie Lewis had attained near-celebrity status in their grade. The girl was all whipped cream and no pudding, as far as Cleo was concerned.

"I'm sure you'll be fantastic." Cleo flourished her flyer while she had the floor. "Speaking of ads, Caylee and I are advertising our new business: Passion Clips! Show them, Caylee."

Caylee flipped up the lid of the sample case and everyone—except Lexie—moved in for a closer look.

"We can make anything—practically. We can put your name on them too. See? Caylee made this one for me." She pointed to the lightbulb in her hair and everyone said how cute and creative it was, except Lexie. She stood just outside the circle, her arms crossed tightly and a pout on her face.

Cleo poured it on. "So, what are you good at? What do you love? Buy Passion Clips for all your hobbies and passions and 'tell the world who you are!' "

Taylor picked out some ballet slippers with pink ribbons. "I've been in ballet since I was five." No surprise there. Taylor was tall and slender and often wore her straight blond hair in a ballerina bun.

"Only four dollars each or seven dollars for two. And we'll put your name on them."

"I don't have any money at school."

"You can bring it Monday."

"Okay. I'll ask my mom. She'll buy me anything ballet."

Lexie hovered, still looking displeased over the loss of the spotlight.

"I was thinking you might like a brush and comb, Mia," Cleo said, pointing to the pictures she'd drawn on the ad. "Since you're so good with hair. You could make those, right, Caylee?"

"Sure."

"I kind of like the chef hat and spoon." She pointed to those drawings. "I've been getting into baking lately."

"Great!" Cleo's ad was working! "What about you, Lexie?" she asked.

"No thanks. Too babyish for—"

"Sunglasses? Purses? I know! Glittering stars for the TV star?" Cleo waggled her eyebrows.

"Stars! Just like the Avenue of the Stars on Hollywood Boulevard!" exclaimed Taylor.

"Exactly!" Cleo wished she'd thought of that, but whatever. Taylor was helping her make the sale. "And with your name on them, they'll look just like those sidewalk stars. Don't you think, Caylee?"

Caylee looked unsure.

"Right, Caylee?" Cleo urged Caylee with her eyes. This was not a good time for one of Caylee's confidence crises.

"Uhh . . . right. Sure."

Lexie rolled her eyes. "Oh, okay. I'll take *one*."

Yes!

"But make sure you spell my name right. Lexie with an *ie*."

Caylee drew a big star with Lexie's name inside it on her order pad.

"You have to center it." Lexie poked the paper. "And use the same font as the actual stars. Oh, and there should be a circled television under my name."

"Oh yeah," Taylor said. "They put a record for musicians and a movie camera for movie stars."

Cleo grinned. "It will look just like the real deal. Don't worry!"

Caylee looked worried. "I'm not sure if I can fit—"

"Anyone else?" Cleo asked before Caylee could say anything to kill the deal. "Look at *this* one." She held up the furry clip Caylee had made in honor of Tye-Dye, her new pet hamster. The eye was a tiny black bead. Everyone oohed and aahed over how adorable it was. Four more girls wanted clips after that, two of them asking for barrettes to match their pets, including one set of guinea pigs.

The whistle blew and the group dispersed. As Cleo and Caylee headed toward Mr. Boring's line, Cleo added up the orders Caylee had written down. Sixteen pairs and one single for a grand total of $116! And this was only the first day!!

"Quack-quack-quack!"

Everyone scrambled for their seats and quieted down, except Cleo, who was excitedly telling her tablemates about her victorious morning of sales.

"Cleopatra Edison Oliver, CEO," Mr. Boring interrupted. "Would you still like to share with the class this latest business you're launching?"

"It's me and Caylee, and I think everyone heard about it over lunch."

"You mean I missed your spiel?"

"My what?"

"You know, your sales pitch, your selling job, your elevator speech . . ."

"Oh! Right." If Mr. Boring bought a pair, other teachers might too. She had almost overlooked an important segment of the market. "Our business is called Passion Clips. We make personalized hair clips in just about any shape, with or without your name, so you can tell the world who you are!"

"How about you, Mr. B?" Cole interjected. "Want a pair?"

"My hair does sometimes get in my eyes." He swiped the hair at the sides of his face. "Seriously though, see me after school, if you have time. I might be interested." A few boys laughed. "For my *daughters.*"

"Ohhhh," they all said.

Yippee! Another order—most likely for more than one pair, since he had said daughters, plural. She gave Caylee a thumbs-up. Caylee smiled in return.

"Thanks, Mr. B. If you buy two pairs"—she scribbled in the margin of her notebook—"we'll have sold thirty-seven clips for a grand total of one hundred and thirty dollars!"

Mr. Boring raised his eyebrows. "Wow. I thought for a minute you were going to say if I ordered two pairs, I'd get a third for half price."

Cleo considered the idea. "I'll need to discuss it with my partner"—she jerked her chin toward Caylee—"but chances are good we could work something out." She was wheelin' and dealin'!

Mr. B smiled. "Great. And now, onto Adventures in Science! with me, your host, Adventurer-Scientist Ted Boring. Today, we're starting a new unit on—drumroll, please—"

All the kids slapped their palms on their desks and thunder rolled through the room. Cleo drummed extra hard, loving every minute she got to make noise in class and not get in trouble for it.

"Bugs!"

A few girls made *ewww* sounds. Micah pulled his elbow into his side with a clenched fist and said, "Yes!" Cleo agreed with Micah. She had never minded bugs and thought girls who said "ewww" to them were kind of silly.

Quentin McDonnell raised his hand. "Can I do my paper on the computer variety?"

"Actually, we won't be writing papers."

Cleo pulled *her* elbow into her side. "Yes!"

"And computer bugs don't fit within the scope of this particular unit."

Quentin's face fell.

"However, you may feel free to write a paper on computer viruses for extra credit any time you like."

Now it was Quentin's turn: "Yes!"

"We'll be looking at insect anatomy, behavior, habitat, roles within their larger ecosystems, life cycles. And we will be doing this by observing one insect in particular." He pushed a button on his computer keyboard and words started zooming onto the smart board. "Of the kingdom Animalia, of the phylum Arthropoda, of the class Insecta—"

Were they going to have to remember all this gobbledygunk?

"—of the order Coleoptera—"

"Ooo, that one's kind of like *my* name!" Cleo blurted, and then slapped her hand over her mouth. She couldn't get another strike.

"Of the family Tenebrionidae . . . the *Tenebrio molitor!*"

"Say what?" said Cole Lewis.

"Mealworms," said Mr. Boring, facing the class.

"Mealworms?" Micah's face screwed up.

"Yes! Their scientific name comes from words that mean"—he made his voice sound spooky—"'One who prowls at night in the ground meal.'"

That sounded pretty cool, but what in the heck was ground meal?

"I'll be giving each of you five to take home and observe over the next two weeks."

Amelie raised her hand. "I can't. I'm allergic to worms."

Max Peacock piped up. "No one's allergic to worms."

"No, really! They make my skin itch."

"First of all," Mr. Boring jumped in, "mealworms aren't worms. They're larvae of the darkling beetle." He pointed to the word that looked sort of like *Cleopatra*. "Second, Amelie, I'll call your parents and we'll make sure it's all cool. Does anyone else have a known allergy to insects?" He scanned the room. "Good. I'll pass them out now and we can start getting to know our new little buddies. Amelie, you can just look at yours through the plastic."

He gave everyone a small, lidded tub filled with what looked like pencil shavings. Mr. B told them it was actually oat bran for the larvae to eat. When he put Cleo's in front of her, she was puzzled. And disappointed. The "prowlers" were about a half inch long, skinny, light brown with darker brown stripes, and smooth, with no visible teeth. Completely harmless-looking. They weren't even slimy.

Cleo raised her hand.

"Yes, Cleo?"

"Do you think someone overdid it a bit with the name? *Tenebrio molitor* makes them sound like something out of a monster movie."

Mr. Boring laughed. "Wait until you look at them through a magnifier"—he held up a lens—"you might see some monster resemblances." He instructed them to take off the lids and pick one out. "Place it on the lid so it can't crawl away. We don't want mealworms getting loose in the school and creating an infestation."

More *ewww*s from around the class. Cleo thought of her family's mouse problem. The traps Dad had bought hadn't caught a thing.

"Invasion of the *Tenebrio molitor*," Cole said in a ghost-announcer voice.

Cleo opened her container. The mealworms were having a squirm party. Their bodies bent this way and that, making *J*s and *U*s in the oat bran. They crawled on one another with dozens of little buggy legs. How was she supposed to pick one up? They were so wiggly.

Micah had one between his fingers already. Its body arced back and forth. He held it up, grinning wildly. A shiver ran down Cleo's back. She didn't want to look like a scaredy-cat, or worse, a priss. But now that she had to touch one, they suddenly gave her the creeps. "Sorry to break up the party, guys," she whispered, then quickly reached in and grabbed one. *Eww!* So squirmy!

"Ahhh!" Micah screamed. Something plopped on Cleo's head. Something SQUIRMY!

Cleo sprung from her chair. "Is it on me? Get it off!" She swatted at her hair but didn't want to smash the worm on her head, so she hurled her braids toward the ground instead. She bent at the waist— down, up, down, up—so fast and hard that her lightbulb clip flew off. Laughter and shouting erupted around her. Mr. Boring quacked his duck call until everyone settled down.

"That little sucker bit me!" Micah said, and stuck his thumb in his mouth.

Mr. Boring stooped at Cleo's feet. When he stood, a mealworm squirmed between his fingers. "Huh. I didn't know they could bite. We've learned something already." He set the bug on Micah's container lid. "Anyway, it looks like he survived the ordeal." He put a hand on Cleo's shoulder. "Will you?"

Cleo shuddered, breathing hard. "I think so." She looked at her empty hands. "My worm!" In her panic, she'd forgotten all about it.

Cole tapped her on the shoulder and pointed to her chair. The worm squirmed its way across. "You almost had a mealworm pancake." He laughed.

She took a deep breath, picked up the bug, and put it on her lid. Then she sat.

"Your goal for the next two weeks is, first of all, to keep them alive." He raised an eyebrow at Cleo and Micah. "And second of all, to learn as much as you can about these little guys. You will be formulating questions and devising experiments—*humane* experiments—to find answers."

While Mr. Boring led them through an exploration of all the parts of a mealworm, Cleo thought about names. She had five new pets to care for. They deserved names.

Their neighbor Miss Jean had named her chickens after the women's rights leaders she admired: Gloria, Alice, Susan B, and Big Betty.

Cleo wouldn't ever *dare* give Fortune's name to a mealworm . . . but how about other successful business moguls and entrepreneurs? She picked up the larva that had almost gotten squashed and looked into its scrunchy little face. "Hello, Steve Jobs." The former Apple founder and CEO may have been a little intense, but he'd also been a marketing genius. "You and me got the bug for business!"

CHAPTER 4

Unzipped

Caylee came home with Cleo that day so they could celebrate their success. "Mom! We got nineteen orders on our first day of business! Will you buy a pair? Please!"

Mom was mixing up a batch of Cleo's Canine Cookies™. The doggie treats had been Cleo's idea—after Mom's healthy cookies turned out to be more popular with Barkley than with people. They planned to sell them at the farmers' market as soon as a space opened up and Mom had enough money to afford the booth-rental fee. For now, she was test-marketing them to the neighbors' dogs.

Cleo grasped her hands under her chin, put on her angel face, and fluttered her eyelids. "If you order, that will bring our total to twenty! And twenty is such a nice, round number." She put her head against her mom's shoulder and gazed up into her eyes.

Mom wiped her hands on her apron. "Wow. That's fantastic!"

"Not just fantastic, Mom. It's fantasta*mazing*! Amazatas-tic! We are one dynamic duo!" Cleo held out her fist and Caylee bumped it with her own, giggling. "Ka-pow!" They fluttered their fingers in the air as they pulled their hands away.

"You sure are," Mom said.

"I've got the *Cleopatra touch*!" Cleo jutted one hand in front and one behind, like Dad when he did the "Walk Like an Egyptian" dance to make them all laugh. She strutted around the kitchen.

"Okay, let's not get carried away . . ."

"What, Mom? We need to celebrate!"

"Maybe we should wait until we've actually made them," Caylee said. "We've got a lot of work to do."

"*Relax*, Cay-Cay. We'll pump them out in no time!"

Caylee's brow creased.

"Ooo, I know! We need a special sparkling drink to toast to our success." Cleo grabbed a Sprite and the red-sticky-sweet grenadine syrup from the fridge. "Shirley Temples all around!"

Mom looked at her through half-closed eyes, eyebrows raised and mouth set. But a smile was there . . . at the corners of her lips and eyes, wanting to take over her whole face.

Josh zoomed into the room. Jay followed closely on his heels. "Did someone say 'Shirley Temples'?"

Mom broke. "Oh, all right. Drinks for everyone!" The boys cheered and Mom sent them back out. "And yes, I'd be happy to buy a pair."

"Thanks, Mom!" Cleo turned to Caylee. "I'll take yellow smiley faces with braces, please. Since I'll be getting mine soon."

Mom planted her fists on her hips. "Hey! Who said I was buying them for *you*? I want a pair for myself!"

Cleo frowned and Caylee laughed. "What do you want to tell the world about who *you* are, Miss Nicki?"

Mom's lips slid to one side of her face. "Hmm. That's

a good question. Definitely *not* anything having to do with hospitals." Mom had worked at Saint Luke's before Cleo's brothers had come. Not as a doctor or nurse. She did something called "risk management." Entrepreneurs had to manage risks too, but they also had to take them, which Mom didn't seem to like as much.

The mention of hospitals somehow reminded Cleo of her mealworms, potentially roasting in her backpack and in need of resuscitation. "Oh! I almost forgot!" She rushed to the front door, where she'd left her bag. The boys crowded around, wanting to know if the Shirley Temples were ready. She pulled out the container. "Back up, everybody. They need some air."

"Who needs air?" Josh asked.

"My mealworms," Cleo answered.

"*Mealworms?*" Mom had just come into the room.

"They're harmless," Cleo said. Barkley sniffed inside her backpack.

Jay pulled on her arm. "Let me see!" Cleo kept the container out of reach and headed for the dining table.

"You didn't like it so much when one landed on your head." Caylee gave a snorty little laugh.

"On your head?" Mom said.

Cleo nodded. "Yeah, Micah threw it when it bit him."

Jay finally backed off.

"They *bite*?" Mom said. "I thought you said they were harmless!"

"I get to do experiments on them."

"Do you get to cut them open?" Josh asked, wild-eyed and grinning.

"*No!* We're supposed to keep them alive." She took off the lid, hoping she hadn't killed them already. Everyone crowded around. The worms squirmed in their huddle. Phew. What would she have done if they'd overheated? Done mouth-to-mouth on the creepy-crawlies? The thought gave *her* creepy-crawlies, but it also made her laugh. She replaced the lid.

Mom shook her head. "First mice. Now mealworms. We've got our own little pest zoo going here."

"You forgot our main exhibit." Cleo's eyes slid to her brothers.

"Cleo . . ." Mom warned.

Caylee got her mealworms and they went to the kitchen for food—for themselves *and* their buggy friends. They decided on grapes. They plopped a couple of grape halves into each of the insect containers and replaced the lids. Then they made their Shirley Temples, dropping in grapes, since they didn't have any maraschino cherries to make them fancy.

Everyone gathered in the dining area to clink glasses. "To our first fabulous day of sales," Cleo said. The boys guzzled their drinks. Mom took a sip. Cleo savored her first swallow and then blurted, "Fortune!" How could she have forgotten?

She and Caylee started for the family room.

"Homework, Cleo?" Mom's one-word question stopped her.

Normally, Cleo wouldn't have any on a Friday. But her conscience poked her about her uncompleted simile assignment. *Pesky conscience.*

She moaned and then tromped back to her backpack. "I'll do it in the family room. It won't take long."

"No TV until it's done," Mom reminded.

"I know!" Cleo kept the worms with her. For now, she'd keep them close—in case her brothers got any crazy ideas.

"I have to finish my similes," she said, settling onto the love seat with the mealworms beside her. "As *quickly* as Fortune makes money. Want to help?"

"Sure." Caylee sat on her left, which was good since Cleo was right-handed. It was a little cramped, but it would work. They put their drinks on the coffee table.

"What word did you choose for yourself?" Cleo asked.

"*Organized*, of course! I'm as organized as a library. I'm as organized as the periodic table. I'm as organized as a filing cabinet."

"Not if you're *my* filing cabinet!"

"You don't have a filing cabinet."

"I'm just saying, if I did." Cleo took a sip of her drink.

"How many do you have left?" Caylee asked.

"All of them."

"*All* of them?"

"I got distracted. But now, I'm as *persistent* as . . ." Cleo began. "A dripping faucet," she said, thinking of the sink in the upstairs bathroom that drove her nuts with its *drip-drip-drip*.

"How about a seed in dirt?" Caylee suggested.

"A seed in *rocky* dirt!" Cleo scribbled it down. She thought some more. What else couldn't be stopped when it was striving after a goal, like her with all her bright ideas? Who else wouldn't give up until they wore down their opponents or overcame all obstacles and got what they wanted? "The Itsy-Bitsy Spider!" she shouted. Jay loved that song—a little too much, Cleo thought.

"Good one," Caylee said. "I had to go to the dentist last week. She sure was persistent about scraping my teeth."

"Ooo yeah. What do they call that tool they use?"

"A scaler, I think."

"I'm as persistent as a dentist with a scaler." They laughed. "Only one more."

Barkley came into the room. He sniffed around on the carpet. His nose led him to Cleo's mealworms. "Don't even think about it," she said, snatching up the container. She set it on the bookshelf behind her, out of Barkley's reach. He looked at her with inquiring eyes, and she rubbed behind his ears. "You can have some lovin' but you can't have my mealworms." Barkley moved over to the bookshelf.

"You could just tell Mr. Boring, 'My dog ate my homework.'" Caylee giggled.

"First it's my *room* . . . then it's my *dog* . . ."

Barkley stood with his paws on the level of the mealworms and continued to sniff the container. "Down, Barkley!" Cleo commanded.

"He sure is being *persistent*," Caylee said.

"Sheesh. I know." *Wait a minute . . .*

Cleo grinned. She wrote her fifth and final simile, "As persistent as a dog that's caught a scent! Thanks, Jelly. And Barkley." He finally came over and lay at their feet. Cleo grabbed the remote and turned on the TV. Hopefully they hadn't missed too much.

Fortune was radiant, as always. Her round eyes sparkled. Cleo felt a magnetic tug toward this woman who looked more like Cleo than anyone in Cleo's family.

Fortune spoke to her studio audience. "As you all know, my personal mission statement is what drives me. And that statement is to . . ."

Everyone, including Cleo, chimed: "Deliver destinies and finance futures!" The audience applauded.

"Yes! And today on my show, I have the opportunity to introduce you to a young woman who has a *for-sure* destiny, people! Breanna Anderson was adopted as a baby by a loving couple."

Cleo's heart began to thump.

"As an older teen, Breanna became life-and-death ill. It turned out she needed . . . a kidney transplant. Having a genetic match would be the best place to find a kidney for her, but she knew very little about her birth parents and all her family's attempts at locating them had failed."

Cleo's heart raced. The sound of it filled her ears, making it hard to focus on what Fortune was saying.

"That's when Breanna's parents did a very daring thing. They got in touch with *me*, which, I admit, is not always the easiest thing to do." The camera cut to audience members nodding and smiling. "But these folks were determined! They would not take no for an answer."

Cleo was filled with dread. Was Fortune about to announce that she'd put a baby up for adoption and the grown-up girl had found her? Was she about to introduce the daughter that Cleo had always dreamed would be *her*?

Fortune went on. "I'm so glad they didn't give up, because they gave me the chance to deliver a destiny by helping them track down Breanna's biological family."

Cleo held her breath.

"Today, I am so pleased to be able to introduce Breanna, with her *new kidney*!" People clapped and cheered. Fortune raised her voice to be heard: "Joining Breanna is her mom, Mrs. Beth Anderson, *and* her *birth* mother, Ms. Shari Jenkins, who gave up a kidney and gained a family. Please help me in welcoming them!" Everyone clapped as the three women walked onto the set.

Cleo locked her arms around her bent knees and pulled them into her chest.

"Wow! Isn't this an amazing story?" Caylee was riveted to the screen.

Cleo just nodded. She felt like clicking off the TV and running outside.

A huge racket erupted in the kitchen. Josh and Julian were at it again. Mom yelled at them. She appeared in the doorway, her hands covered in canine cookie goop. "Cleo, I know you're watching your show, but please do me a huge favor and take your brothers outside. I'm about to lose it with them." She rushed back out, saying, "You can record it!"

Cleo jumped up and turned off the TV. "Come on, Caylee."

Caylee glanced toward the dark screen, looking disappointed. "They were right in the middle of that great interview."

Cleo shrugged. "The work of a big sister is never done." She smiled, feeling the falseness of her attempt to sound normal.

They went to the kitchen, where Josh and Jay rolled around on top of each other like something you'd see in a cartoon.

"Are you recording it?" Mom asked over the crying and screaming.

Cleo shook her head. "Nah, that's okay."

Fortunately, Mom was too busy pulling the boys apart to question why Cleo wasn't recording her absolute-favorite show.

As soon as Cleo mentioned baseball, her brothers were racing to the front door. The whole time they played, Cleo tried not to think about the mothers and daughter she'd seen on *Fortune*, but the story had unzipped her insides. She grasped the edges of her feelings and held on tightly, trying to keep everything from falling out.

CHAPTER 5

Persist and Prevail

Saturday morning, Mom was on her again about keeping her room neat. Only a couple of days had passed since Caylee had helped her completely clean it, but a lot could happen in two days. Heck, Cleo's room could be turned upside down in a matter of minutes!

She picked up the piles that had multiplied faster than the fruit flies hovering around her trash can, and shoved them into desk drawers and the closet. Suddenly, she was thinking about her birth mom again. What did *her* bedroom look like, Cleo wondered. Was it something out of

Better Homes and Gardens (a magazine full of rich people's houses Mom sometimes bought at the store) or was it more like the hazard zone around Cleo's feet? Was being neat and tidy something you got from your genes?

She pushed a pile of homework papers under the bed, ignoring Fortune staring at her from the poster on the wall.

She knew she wasn't abiding by Fortune Principle Number Eight for How to Build Your Business and Live the Life You Want: *Shortcuts sell you and your customers short.* But she had to go fast. She and Caylee had a ton of barrettes to make!

She checked on her new pets. The grapes had dried up overnight, but fortunately the worms hadn't. She couldn't tell if the grapes had been eaten or if they were just smaller from shriveling. She scribbled a note on the food log Mr. Boring had suggested they make: *Grapes— eaten or shrivelled?*

Did *shrivelled* have one *l* or two? She didn't know and she didn't care. Much more crucial was how to tell the bugs apart when they looked exactly the same.

She opened the desk drawer where she'd just dumped her fingernail polishes.

Five colors. Five bugs.

Perfect.

She opened a bottle of polish and put a dot of color—Candied Apple Red—on the first worm's behind (she made sure it was the behind—she didn't want to blind them). She made a small mark with the polish in the journal where she was recording her observations. After the red color she wrote, = Zoë Nylon. Ms. Nylon ran a fashion empire.

The designer Trudy Ferretti got a pink behind. Tiara Humbird, CEO of Happy Gorilla, Inc., a worldwide toy and gaming conglomerate, got purple. Restaurateur Ronald Vanderpump's rump was gold. And Steve Jobs got green. She had no idea which ones were actually girls and which were boys. They didn't seem to have any of the parts that let you know which was which.

"Now I can keep track of you! So, what do you feel like eating today?" She had another flash of inspiration. "Wait here! I'll be right back. You're not going to believe how tasty this next treat is!"

She rushed downstairs to the kitchen. Mom wasn't there. She could just sneak what she wanted. But Mom would notice, eventually. And then she'd have to listen *again* to the lecture about taking things without asking, and probably lose out on something she wanted, like going to Caylee's. She poked her head into the living room. "Mom, can I get a Kit Kat from the cupboard? For the worms, I mean. Although they're not actually worms. They're larvae."

Mom grimaced. "Kit Kat? I don't think worms *or* larvae are going to eat a Kit Kat."

Dad looked up from the table where he and the boys were building LEGO sets. "I know who *would*." He winked at Cleo. *Rats*. He'd seen through her plan, but that wouldn't stop Miss Itsy-Bitsy!

"We don't have Kit Kats, anyway," Mom said.

"Yes, we do." Cleo went to the kitchen, dragged the footstool, and opened the cabinet over the stove. She reached behind the jars and bottles of cooking oils and plucked out the six-pack of Kit Kats she'd recently discovered. One had been eaten already, but not by her. She'd been waiting for the right time to reveal she knew they were there. And this was it.

When she reappeared, Mom turned pink. "Oh . . . I forgot about those."

Jay stopped building as soon as he saw the candy. "Can I have one?"

"Me too!" Josh said.

"Don't forget about me and Steve Jobs." Cleo held the Kit Kats above her brothers' grabbing hands.

"Steve Jobs?" Dad asked.

"I named my mealworms after inspirational entrepreneurs. Except Fortune, of course. I could never give that *fantabulous* name to a worm."

"Funny thing," Dad said. "I just read something about how insects, like your little larvae, could be the solution to world hunger. Lots of people already eat them as a regular part of their diet, including mealworms."

"People eat bugs?" Josh said, wrinkling his nose. "On *purpose*? Gross!"

Cleo agreed. The thought of a mealworm wriggling around in her mouth or biting down on its squishy body made her gag. And *not* metaphorically.

"Did you know there are forty tons of bugs for each person on the planet?" Dad said.

"Forty *tons*?" Mom sounded disbelieving.

"Yep. That's a lot of food we're missing out on, huh? Great source of protein . . . and I've heard they taste sort of nutty."

Cleo thought her dad was nutty. "I'd rather have a Kit Kat," she said.

"Me too!" Jay shouted.

Cleo locked eyes with her mom.

"Oh, all right. That's what I get for trying to hide them. I'll be happy to see them gone. Lord knows I don't need the temptation."

"Why did you buy them if you didn't want to eat them?" Cleo handed her the package.

"Good question, Cleo," Dad said, smiling at Mom as she ripped the candy wrapper open, broke it up, and handed the kids each a bar, keeping the last one for herself.

"We all do things that aren't good for us," she muttered, and took a bite.

Cleo shoved the whole bar into her mouth at once. "How about one for the larva entrepreneurs?"

"You were supposed to share that one!" Mom said. "They don't need a whole bar."

"Maybe they don't. But I do!" Cleo grinned, still chewing.

"What if the chocolate makes them sick—or kills them?"

"I guess I'll discover they shouldn't eat candy."

Mom sighed. "They and me both." She opened another bar.

Yes! Cleo had persisted and prevailed. "Thanks, Mom! Remember, you're advancing science!"

Mom swatted at her with the package of remaining Kit Kats, but Cleo moved too quickly for her. Candy in hand, she ran upstairs to try food experiment number two. She chomped down on the bar and enjoyed her half (or maybe three-fourths) while she crumbled the rest into the container. "Here you go, little buggies. I'll be back later this afternoon to see what you thought of it."

She looked up at Fortune again. The mom on yesterday's show had persisted until she got what she wanted too. Fortune had found the girl's birth mom and saved her life.

Cleo suddenly knew what she had to do. She had to get Fortune's attention, by whatever means possible. She had told Caylee she wanted to be on Fortune's show one day. Why not now? Getting herself, or even just her product, on Fortune's show would be the hugest break ever.

She would persist until she prevailed!

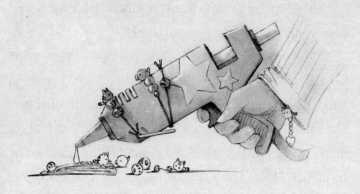

CHAPTER 6

Missing Pictures

Only two houses separated Cleo's house from her best friend's glorious pink villa with the Spanish-style, red-tiled roof. Cleo ran past Miss Jean's and the Williamses'. She didn't have time to get caught up in conversation with the neighbors. Fortunately, no one was outside.

She ran up Caylee's painted front steps, smooth and emerald green, and grabbed the lion's head door-knocker. *Knock-knock-knock.* Standing in front of their giant wooden door, she felt like Dorothy seeking entrance to the Land of Oz. No one ever opened the little window behind the knocker, although she had tried it once, just to see what it felt like to be inside such an opulent house looking out. She'd had to stand on a chair, of course.

Caylee opened the door. "Hi, Peanut Butter."

"Didn't your mom teach you to ask who it is?"

"No one else uses the knocker. Why don't you use the doorbell, Ding Dong?"

"I like the knocker. It can't be ignored." She stepped inside and slipped off her shoes. "And if I'm a Ding Dong, then you're a Twinkie."

"Okay, Ding Dong." Caylee smiled and then yawned.

Cleo suppressed the urge to yawn in return. This was no time to be tired! They needed to be productive!

They headed down the hall. Cleo noticed spaces on the walls where framed photos of Caylee's family used to hang. Those pictures probably weren't coming back, now that her dad was getting remarried. Thinking about Caylee's dad just up and leaving his family made Cleo's stomach feel quivery. It was the same feeling she got during earthquake aftershocks—those little reminders that the place where they lived had some big cracks in it.

Caylee yawned again as they climbed the stairs.

"Didn't you get enough sleep?" Cleo asked.

"It's Tye-Dye . . . he woke me up super early, running in his wheel thingy."

"I finally get to meet your hamster!" Mrs. Ortega had gotten the pet at the recommendation of the counselor who was helping Caylee cope with the changes in her family. "So how is he? Other than a morning person—I mean, hamster."

"Technically, he's crepuscular."

"Huh?"

"Most active at dawn and dusk. Although I think he might be nocturnal too, because he makes a *lot* of noise in the middle of the night. But he's good. Still getting used to me, I think." She yawned yet again as she opened her bedroom door.

Caylee's room was completely ordered, organized, and color-coordinated—mostly in shades of blue and aqua. Not a crumb-covered plate or food wrapper in sight. Nothing on the floor except a plastic tablecloth covering the circular floor rug, and towers of plastic drawers full of crafting stuff. *Organized* crafting stuff.

Cleo zoomed to the large plastic bin on the other side of the room. She sat on the floor and looked inside the wire-mesh window. Shredded paper covered the floor of the bin. There was a plastic, aqua-colored exercise wheel; a plastic, blue-and-aqua mini-playground with tunnels and a tower; and, in one corner, a small, furry mass of brown, tan, and white splotches curled up in a nest of toilet paper.

"What a cutesy-wutesy! Can I hold him?"

Caylee peered through the mesh rectangle in the lid of the bin. "You don't want to. He's cranky when he wakes up."

Cleo smirked. "Sounds like Josh."

"You have to give them at least a half hour to eat, drink, and potty before trying to interact."

"Yep. Never talk to Josh in the morning, especially when he's on the toilet."

"And you can't hold them too much or they get stressed out. Like a couple of times a day for ten minutes."

"That's it?"

"Yeah, but they like to play. Check this out!" Caylee held up a see-through plastic ball, the size of a large cantaloupe. "You put them inside this and they run around your house."

"Ooo! I want one!"

"A hamster?"

"No. The ball. People-sized!"

Caylee laughed. "The woman at the pet store said I should try to think of a bunch of different activities for him so he doesn't get bored."

"I can definitely help you with that." Cleo grinned. "They don't call me Cleo-I've-Got-an-Idea-Oliver for nothing! What do you feed him?"

"Just some stuff we bought at the store." She held up a bag with the words *Hamster Hash* written across the front. "The pet store lady said he'll probably need some extra protein, like egg, cheese, and you'll never guess what else."

"What?"

"Mealworms!"

"You could tell Mr. Boring, 'My *hamster* ate my homework!'" They laughed. "My dad told me this morning that some *people* eat mealworms. Like, as actual food."

Caylee cringed. "Ew."

"I know. Not to mention, I'm getting kind of attached to my little larvae. I could never eat Zoë or Tiara."

"You named your mealworms?"

Cleo opened her eyes wide. "You named your glue gun!"

Caylee picked up her glue gun from its spot on her crafting table and hugged it to her chest. "My Gloopy," she said in a dreamy voice.

"You're such a dork!"

Caylee batted her eyelashes. "The dork you love the most."

"It's true. Hey, can I see your iPad?" Cleo asked. The tablet, in its leopard-spotted cover, sat on Caylee's desk.

"Sure. I don't care about that nearly as much as I care about Gloopy."

Cleo tapped the screen until she found what she was looking for: The New York Stock Exchange. She entered Fortune Enterprises, Inc.'s three-letter symbol: FEI. Share values were up by two percent. Not too shabby.

"Do you understand all that?" Caylee pointed to a line graph that looked like a craggy mountain range with all of its ups and downs.

"I understand that it ends on a peak, and that's what matters," Cleo replied.

"Ooo! Let me show you something cool I did last night!" Caylee reached for the tablet.

Cleo returned to the home screen and handed it over.

Caylee tapped on an icon and a list appeared. "I created an inventory of all my craft supplies."

Cleo looked over her shoulder. "You've got forty-two ink pads? And twenty-seven jars of glitter?"

"You can never have too much glitter."

"What's a die cutter? It sounds kind of violent."

"They're for paper cutting. Like a hole punch, but different shapes. Not violent at all."

"Unless you're a piece of paper," Cleo said. "You have *thirty-seven* of them?"

"Yeah. Flowers, footprints, hearts, all kinds of animals. My favorite is my iguana."

"Is that how you made me that 'Iguana be a long two weeks without you' card?" Caylee had given the card to Cleo before leaving for her dad's new house in Palm Springs, the last two weeks of summer. Caylee nodded.

"That was your best one yet."

"Thanks. I liked it too."

"What other lists do you have on there?"

"Let's see . . . books I've read, books I want to read, foods I can make, foods I want to learn how to make, places I want to visit, favorite songs, colleges I want to apply to —"

"Colleges? Isn't that kind of a ways off?"

"You can't start thinking about college too early. You've got to plan ahead these days. It's expensive."

Not that Caylee had to worry about that.

"Plus, you have to build up your résumé—activities, community service, achievements. It's gotten really competitive. Your dad should know—he teaches high school."

"I don't even know if I'll go to college."

"*What?* You have to go to college, PB!"

"Why? Lots of successful entrepreneurs never finish college, and they make millions."

"It's still important to get a degree—for job security."

"I'll make my own job security—by running my own companies!" They would have to agree to disagree about this, because Cleo wasn't changing her mind. She looked at the names of Caylee's other lists. "What's 'Kids' Names' for?"

"Possible names for my future children, of course."

"Your *children?*"

"Uh-huh. My top names are Athena for a girl and Asher for a boy."

Cleo smacked her forehead with her palm. "*Cay-Cay!*" Cleo liked to dream about the future too, but all her dreaming had to do with how she was going to make her first million—nothing about kids, unless she was thinking about how to sell stuff to them. Speaking of which, they really should be getting busy making clips. "What's that one?" she asked, pointing to a list titled "Relatives."

"Oh, that's the names of all my relatives. I try to pray for them. I usually forget—until mass." Her lips stretched wide as if she'd just confessed to a horrible deed. "Our priest would call that a 'sin of omission.'"

"What's that mean?" Cleo asked.

"It's like when the wrong that you do is what you *didn't* do."

"Hmm." Just keeping track of the wrong things she *did* do was enough for Cleo. Mom and Dad would most likely agree. "Can I see it?" she asked.

"Sure." Caylee tapped on the title.

Cleo read down the list, a lump forming in her throat. Everything dropped away except that long list of names. These were Caylee's family members. Blood relatives. Caylee could look at them and see bits of herself. She could find herself in stories she heard about Abuelita Cuca or Aunt Luisa. This was not something Cleo could do. Her parents didn't look anything like her. But Mom and Dad were her mom and dad. She had no others.

She didn't really want any others. Her parents loved her. A lot. And yet lately she'd felt a growing desire to know more about her birth parents. To have a relatives list of her own. To see herself in her family. To have some clues about what she might look like all grown-up.

"Can I tell you something?" she said. "But you have to promise not to tell anyone."

Caylee's perfectly arched eyebrows pulled together, making her already-intense eyes look even more so. "Okay." She sounded serious.

Cleo bit on her bottom lip. Was she really going to say this out loud? "Sometimes I wonder if Fortune could be my birth mom."

Caylee pulled her chin into her neck. "Fortune? Really?" Her eyes grew wide. "Do you really think she could be?"

Cleo shook her head. "No." A sharp pain tweaked her heart. "But . . . I like to pretend. And she always talks about how she has this fascination with pharaohs, which made me think, maybe . . ."

"Right." Caylee opened a drawer on one of her crafting towers and pulled out baggies holding felt pieces she'd already cut.

"Don't tell anyone. Remember, you promised."

Caylee looked at her solemnly. "I won't. I promise." She closed the drawer. "So . . . do you ever wonder where your mom and dad *are*?"

Caylee undoubtedly meant her birth parents. Cleo would turn Caylee's little mistake into a joke. "Are you kidding?" She gave a little laugh. "My mom doesn't go to the *bathroom* without letting us know where she is."

Caylee's face turned pink. "I meant . . . your *real* mom and dad."

Something snapped inside Cleo. "My parents *are* my real mom and dad." She felt like Barkley when a stranger came too near to JayJay.

"Oh, sorry. That was dumb." Caylee rushed to her crafting table. She plugged in Gloopy. It was quiet. Caylee rubbed a piece of felt between her fingers. "I'm sorry, Cleo. I wasn't sure how to ask." She faced Cleo again. "It's just that, after Fortune's show yesterday . . . I was just wondering. If you ever think about where your, where your . . ."

"Where my birth parents are?" Cleo helped her. Caylee didn't know any better. Still, it had touched a nerve.

"Right. Your *birth* parents."

How would she answer? Would she tell Caylee the

truth? That she had memorized every last non-identifying detail from the agency's paperwork, which wasn't much, but still, was all she had? Or that she had spent hours gazing at the one and only photograph of her as a baby in her birth mom's arms, her birth mom's head chopped off to keep her face from being seen?

"It's okay," Cleo said finally. "I know we never really talk about it."

Caylee exhaled, nodding. "Thanks." She glued a mane onto a horse body. That would be Tessa's.

"But since we *are* talking about it," Cleo began, "I actually had an idea . . . after seeing that girl and her birth mom on *Fortune* yesterday."

"What is it?" Caylee put the glue gun in its stand and gave Cleo her full attention.

"I want to make Fortune a personalized pair of Passion Clips. I'm going to get on her show, Jelly. Not later. Now."

Caylee's eyes got big again. "Wow. That's . . ."

"Awesome. I know!" Cleo gripped Caylee's arm. "But they have to be *perfect*!"

"Of course. Do you know what you want them to look like?"

"I've been thinking about it. A dollar sign would be

too obvious. And I don't think her passion is money, anyway. But she *is* powerful. And there's her interest in pharaohs. She's always talking about her pharaoh hound, Omar."

"We could send her dog clips that look like her dog."

"Maybe . . ."

"Ooo, I know! How about those death masks that they put on mummies? Like King Tut!"

"I was thinking pyramids —"

"Which are also pictured on a dollar bill!" Caylee exclaimed.

"And, more important, will remind her of a girl named after a pharaoh." She poked her thumbs into her chest. "Me!"

Caylee grabbed Gloopy. She snapped a clear glue stick into place. "Ahhh . . . such a satisfying *click*. Let's get to work."

"Yes! We've got twenty orders to fill, and a super-duper special pair for Fortune. Not to mention all the orders I'm going to get tomorrow."

Caylee looked at her quizzically.

"Pastor is letting me announce our business at church!"

"Woo-hoo!"

They spent the next few hours gluing and decorating clips. For a break, they put Tye-Dye in his hamster ball, walked him to the first floor (so he wouldn't accidentally hurtle down the stairs to an untimely death), and chased him around the house. Cleo left Caylee's flying high, trying hard not to notice the missing pictures as she went.

CHAPTER 7

The Lord Loves a Cheerful Buyer

"Mom!" Cleo called from her closet. The clothes on the floor surrounded her like quicksand. With every shirt she pulled from a hanger, she sank deeper and deeper.

Mom was in her own bedroom down the hall. They were all getting ready for church. "Please don't yell at me from across the house!"

"Where's my purple sweater shirt?" Cleo dug through the pile of clothes on the floor.

Mom didn't answer.

Cleo tromped down the hall. Dad was in their bathroom, shaving. Mom stood in the middle of the room getting dressed. "Do you know where my purple sweater shirt is?"

"Which purple sweater shirt, honey?"

"My *only* purple sweater shirt. With the plaid cuffs and collar that looks like two shirts in one. And the matching skirt. I need it for my presentation. It's my most professional outfit."

"If that's the case, it should be hanging on a hanger in your closet." Mom raised an eyebrow.

Cleo spun and huffed back to her room. Couldn't her mom be a little more helpful? She picked up her container of mealworms and peered in through the side. "Did *you* see where I put that shirt?" Chunks of bran-covered Kit Kat sat untouched. She couldn't believe these worms. Passing up perfectly good chocolate. She'd have to put a carrot stick in before they left for church. She didn't want to be the cause of Ronald Vanderpump's—or any of the others'—demise!

What had she been doing? Oh yes. Her purple sweater shirt. She couldn't give up. She opened her dresser and plucked things out one by one, adding them to the stew of magazines, half-finished drawings and doodles, dolls with tangled hair and pen tattoos, and food wrappers.

By the time Mom appeared at the door, Cleo stood ankle-deep in pants, leggings, shirts, and sweaters. Clothes covered every square inch from the closet to her dresser. "Cleo! What are you doing?"

The last thing she found in her drawer was her skirt. "Here's *one* thing I'm looking for!" She went back to the clothes on hangers to paw through them again. She plucked another shirt off its hanger and added it to the swamp.

"Cleo, no!"

"Oh." A plaid cuff stuck out from between two dresses that had been clinging to each other. "Found it!"

Mom groaned. "Well, I suppose this will give you a chance to reorganize your wardrobe."

Cleo put on the skirt and zipped it up. "Sure. Every company needs a good reorg now and then, and so does every room! Maybe Caylee can come over later and help."

"Why would she do that? She just helped you clean it up the other day!"

"It's just what she does, Mom. Fish swim. Hamsters run around in those little wheelie things. And Caylee organizes. That's why she's my Chief Operating Officer. We all have our 'thing.'"

Mom walked away, shaking her head.

"*I* start businesses!" Cleo called after her. Could she really be expected to keep her room spotless when she had an empire to build? And why did Mom even care? It was *her* room. She was the one who had to live in it. She looked at the huge mess she'd made and then at Fortune, who smiled warmly, her arms always open wide. "Did you have to keep your room clean when you were a kid?" she asked the poster.

Fortune wasn't going to answer, and even if she could, she couldn't help Cleo clean up the catastrophe around her. Her persistence had paid off; she'd found what she was after. But what a mess she'd made in the process.

Driving to church, Cleo thought about the Passion Clips for Fortune and the letter she would write . . . Would she ask Fortune to help her find her birth parents like that girl Breanna and her parents had? She glanced at Mom and

Dad in the front seats. A twinge in her heart told her she shouldn't, she didn't need to. She had her parents. But something else—a gnawing, like hunger, except it wasn't in her stomach—told her that something was missing. She just wanted to know: Did they remember her, think about her, wonder about her too?

Dad parked the minivan in the church lot and they all clambered out. New Beginnings Baptist Church was an oldish building with smooth, white outside walls that made it look like a giant marzipan cake. It was in Altadena Heights, about a mile from where Cleo's family lived, which meant they could walk, but only if they left a half hour before church started, which hardly ever happened, and Cleo was just fine with that. Anyway, it was usually too hot to walk, especially in church clothes. If it wasn't too hot, it might be raining. And sitting for two hours in a church pew damp—whether from perspiration or rain—was no good. Surely, God would agree with Cleo on that.

She grabbed the case of barrettes Caylee had brought by earlier that morning and scanned the lot for Auntie Sabina, her godmother and basketball coach. Auntie Sabina, who became Coach Glover during basketball season, had coached Cleo's team for the last few years through Altadena Heights Park and Rec. Cleo had hoped to make Auntie Sabina her first church customer, but her Toyota Prius wasn't in the parking lot.

In the lobby, Mother Williams welcomed people and handed out bulletins. Mr. and Mrs. Williams lived just a couple of houses up from Cleo's family. Their granddaughter, Tasha, braided Cleo's hair.

"There are my babies!" Mother Williams crowed when she saw Cleo and her brothers. Mrs. Williams's bottom half might have moved slowly but her arms and hands could snatch a person as quick as a mousetrap.

Cleo and Josh let her wrap them in her fleshy arms, but JayJay flitted about trying to avoid getting kissed. Silly kid. It was no use. Mother Williams's arm shot out. She reeled Jay in and planted a giant smooch on his cheek. He grimaced and wiped his face. She laughed, her belly shaking like a bouncy house full of kids. "Oh, I just *love* me some JayJay. And Jesus loves you too. *All* of you." She eyed Mom and Dad. "Even if you don't get here early for Sunday school."

Mom's cheeks got a little pinker than usual. "I'm sure

ber the days of little kids and getting everyone door."

"Mm-hmm, baby. I sure do. And we were in Sunday school every week. No exceptions. We need to train our children up in the way they should go. Amen?"

Mom got as stiff as the clothes that hung on Mrs. Williams's backyard line. "And aren't we glad that God's way is to show mercy and grace?" Mom was edging dangerously close to contradicting the older woman.

Dad cleared his throat and nudged Mom forward, but Mother Williams stepped in front of her. "Ain't that the truth!" She wrapped her arms around Mom, whose eyes opened wide in surprise. Finally, with everyone hugged, they were free to go to their seats.

Mom and Dad moved on with the boys, but Cleo had a potential customer standing right in front of her. "Your hair looks very nice today, Mother Williams," she said, putting to work Fortune Principle Number Seven: *Compliments win customers.*

"Well, that's kind of you to say, Cleo."

Cleo pulled one of her new business cards from her sweater pocket. She had made it on the computer the day before. Dad had taken her to OfficeMax to get them copied onto cardstock.

"I think a Passion Clip would be the perfect final touch."

Mother Williams peered at the card. She took it in her hand.

"Maybe crosses," Cleo suggested. "Or musical notes! I know you love to sing."

"*Passion Clips.* Doesn't that sound exciting? Okay, baby. Maybe after church." She was moving Cleo on with her flyswatter hands, looking past her to the people lining up for their bulletins.

Cleo knew not to push in a situation like this. To make a sale, you needed to have a person's undivided attention, and as long as Mother Williams was welcoming saints into the house of God, she was not going to focus anywhere else.

Cleo entered the sanctuary, headed for the Oliver family pew. It didn't have their name on it, but it might as well have. They sat there every week—two rows from the back on the right-hand side. Dad always said he wanted to be closer to the action, but Mom said that with three kids, being near an exit was *imperative*, which Cleo figured must mean something like "nonnegotiable," because Mom had never budged, and they had never sat anywhere except that row for as long as Cleo could remember. And that was a long time. Her parents had been coming to this church since she was a baby.

Cleo's two best church friends walked in behind their parents. Faith Sullivan was ten like Cleo; Hope was eight. Their little sister Charity was four, same as Jay. "Can I sit with Faith and Hope's family?"

Mom waved at Mrs. Sullivan. "Will it keep you from paying attention?"

"Probably."

Mom laughed. "Well, I must be doing something right. My daughter's honest, at least."

"*Please*, Mom? I won't be disrespectful." If she had a hundred dollars for every time Mom lectured her and her brothers about the importance of showing respect at New Beginnings Baptist Church, she'd be as rich as Fortune. *"Promise."*

"All right. I know you'll do a wonderful job telling everyone about your business."

Cleo stood and looked around the filling sanctuary. For the first time that morning, her stomach felt fluttery. She was excited to tell everyone about her and Caylee's great product, but it *was* a big audience. At least a hundred people. Maybe a hundred and fifty. She would imagine she was Fortune with her studio audience. The thought gave her a burst of confidence.

"Yeah, go get 'em, champ," Dad added, grasping the back of her neck as she squeezed by.

She approached the Sullivans' pew. "Hi, Faith. Hi, Hope. Can I sit with you?"

"Hi, Cleo!" they said.

Mr. and Mrs. Sullivan greeted her and they all shifted over a space to make room. She was just about to open her case to show them the clips when the music started and Brother Gerald, the music leader, got on the microphone. "Good morning, New Beginnings family!"

"Good morning," the crowd echoed.

"This is the day the Lord has made! Turn to your neighbor and say, 'This is the day.'"

Cleo snuck a look at Faith. They giggled.

"This is the day!" everyone else shouted.

"I will rejoice and be glad in *him*!" Brother Gerald exclaimed. Around the church came shouts of "Amen!" and "Yes, sir!" and "Hallelujah!" Now the piano, drum, and bass players played in full force, and everyone was standing, and Brother Gerald and the other singers up front began to sing, "'This is the day . . . this is the day! That the Lord has made . . . that the Lord has made. I will rejoice . . . I will rejoice. And be glad in it . . . and be glad in it!'"

A few ladies around the church played tambourines. They hit the rims and faces of those round circles and filled the air with jingles and pops that punctuated the songs with exclamation marks. They whacked the heck out of those things and never seemed to tire of it. Cleo had asked Miss Gaye-Lynn for tambourine lessons and she was making progress, but her arm wore out long before a song ever ended. Of course, they sang songs for a very long time at New Beginnings Baptist Church.

Cleo didn't mind. When they sang, they stood. And

clapped. And swayed. And raised their arms. And wiggled around. They even sometimes stomped. In other words, Cleo wasn't having to hold her body still or be quiet, as long as they were singing.

Another song began: "'Victory is mine, victory is mine, victory today is mine!'" Cleo thought of herself standing there with the Sullivan family and, as she sometimes did, allowed herself to imagine what it would be like to be *in* their family—with two black parents. And black aunts and uncles and cousins and grandparents. And the thought pinched her heart just hard enough that she didn't want to think about it anymore, but for the rest of the singing time she pretended that they *were* her family. Of course, she would never tell her parents that she did this. It was her own little secret.

Eventually, the singing came to an end. This was when the torturous sitting began. But it would not be as bad today because soon she would get to stand and tell everyone about her business. She would leave this morning with more orders, more customers!

Two deacons came forward to make announcements. This and that meeting was mentioned, and Bible study on Wednesday nights, and they exhorted everyone not to forget about daily prayer at 6:00 a.m.—*6:00 a.m.!*—because all great saints started the day on their knees. Fortune probably would be impressed with such discipline, but Cleo didn't have the will to get up that early. She doubted she ever would.

Finally, they handed things over to Pastor Stubblefield. Was *this* when she would get to speak? "As many—No, I'm sure *all* of you know, we have a very enterprising young lady in our congregation." Cleo beamed from her pew. "Cleopatra Oliver has an announcement to make."

Cleo shot up like a firecracker. She strode confidently toward the pulpit, but climbing the steps her legs started to wobble. She grasped the case tightly to her chest and turned to face the congregation. She smiled big, even though her heart hammered so hard she almost expected to hear it knocking against the plastic carrier.

Then she saw Mr. Williams—"Grandpa Williams," as she and her brothers called him—sitting with the deacons in the front row. His eyes sparkled with pride and his smile said, *Show 'em what you got!* Once again, she felt like her normal, bold self, comfortable with the limelight. She took the handheld microphone from Pastor Stubblefield and set the case on the ground.

"My friend Caylee and I have started a new business, Passion Clips. She'd be here, but she goes to Saint Bart's over on Lake Avenue." People nodded understandingly. She went on, talking faster and faster, her free hand gesturing wildly. She grabbed the case, eager to unveil their product and wow everyone.

She tugged on the latch, but trying to hold the microphone and open the case at the same time was awkward, and the latch wasn't giving. Just as Pastor Stubblefield stepped forward to help, she yanked as hard as she could. The carrier flipped forward, catapulting every single clip through the air. People in the front row ducked or held up their hands, trying to avoid getting hit in the face.

Cleo stood, stunned.

Grandpa Williams bent over and picked up Mia's chef hat barrette, which had landed at his feet. He used his dog-handled walking stick to push himself to standing, looking at the barrette the whole time. Finally, he held the barrette in the air. "Talk about craftsmanship! Ooo-ee!" He ran his hand over his balding head. "These clips are so fantastic, even the follicly-challenged, like me, will want to wear them!" Laughter sounded around the church. He clipped the puffy white hat to the lapel of his suit coat.

"And we make them to order," Cleo reminded every-one. "So you can tell the world who you are!"

"How about barbecued ribs?" Grandpa Williams was famous for his mouthwatering barbecue. "Could you make me a baby back ribs barrette to go with this chef's hat?" People hooted and hollered some more.

"Sure! And only seven dollars for the pair," she added.

"For *two* one-of-a-kind handmade pieces of art like this? Folks, that's a bargain right there."

People nodded around the church.

"And we're giving away ten percent of our profits to help orphans go to school in other countries."

Cleo was about to start picking up clips, but Pastor Stubblefield grasped her shoulder. He had the mic again. "Glory to God! This young woman has already learned the value of tithing. Now listen, we need to support the young people in our community. Especially young entre-preneurs! Everyone here can afford to buy at least one clip from this lovely young lady. You've heard 'The Lord loves a cheerful giver'? Well, in this case, the Lord will also love a cheerful buyer!"

Everyone applauded. A few people shouted, "Amen!" Cleo scrambled around, picking up barrettes. With others helping, it took only a minute and she was back in her seat between Mom and Dad, where she belonged.

Grandpa Williams turned around and winked at her. She winked back, wishing that he were her real grandpa.

CHAPTER 8

Building the Buzz

Monday morning, Caylee came over before school to package the barrettes they'd completed over the weekend. They had finished all of the school orders Sunday afternoon, but hadn't even started on the twenty-eight church orders. Fortune's special-edition pyramid clips would be done by that evening, Caylee promised. She needed a special gold glitter spray paint to finish the job, which her mom had agreed to pick up on her way home.

Cleo inspected their work. The clips were packaged in small, sheer drawstring bags Mom had bought but never used, a business card in each one. *Perfect.*

"Off to deliver to our customers!" Cleo kissed Mom on the cheek and hoisted her backpack full of orders onto her shoulders.

"And go to school, right?" Mom said, smiling. "You remember that little thing called 'school'?"

"Of course!" Cleo said, pushing past the screen door. She felt like running all the way there. "See you after *school*, when we'll all be a little richer!"

Cleo and Caylee walked side by side. Josh, his LA Dodgers cap secure on his head, followed behind.

"Ooo, I can't wait to hand people their clips!" Cleo said. "I hope after they see these first ones, they'll want to *add* to their collection." She waggled her eyebrows.

"What Passion Clips would be in your collection to tell the world who *you* are?" Caylee asked.

"I bet I could come up with a hundred of them!"

"A hundred?"

"Sure. I've got a lot to say!"

"You need a barrette with a mouth on it."

Cleo nodded emphatically. "Definitely. It's the key to my superpower. I think I should have a pair of mouths."

"Uh, two mouths on *you* would be dangerous."

Cleo flicked Caylee's shoulder. "Hey!"

"Just joking." Caylee grinned.

"And you should have a pair of ears—"

"I already do!"

Cleo stuck out her tongue. "Ear *barrettes*, silly! Because you're a great listener."

"Awww. Thanks."

Cleo went back to imagining her Passion Clips collection. Her lips squished to one side and then the other. Her forehead bunched with the effort of turning "who she was" into things that could go on barrettes. It was kind of like making up similes in class.

She was all about starting businesses. An entrepreneur. But how could that be shown with a hair clip? As with Fortune, money wasn't *the* most important thing to her (although it was still important). What she loved was the thrill of having an idea and seeing it turn into something real. Having something that others wanted. That's what she liked about doing business.

"What about basketballs?" Caylee prompted. "You love to play basketball, and you're good at it too."

"Ooo, and jerseys for the LA Sparks—my favorite WNBA team. My favorite team, period."

"I think you should have tornados," Caylee said.

"Tornados?"

"Yeah, because you're sort of a force of nature, you know. You make an impact wherever you go."

Cleo considered that. She'd never thought of herself as a "force of nature." She liked it though.

"You also leave a huge mess!" Caylee grinned again.

Josh started making kissing sounds. "I'm telling everyone your business is called Passion *Lips*!"

"Fine by me." Cleo picked up the pace. The school was in sight. "Any press is good press, as far as I'm concerned." She had another thought. "Hey, Josh! You just gave me a great idea! After we get Passion Clips up and running, we could add a line of personalized lip balms. Passion Lips! Mixing flavors based on customers' requests!"

"Ooo . . . I'd want cherry bubblegum," Caylee said. "Or maybe peach cream soda."

"Pineapple peppermint! Chili lime! Strawberry cinnamon!" Cleo added. "The possibilities would be endless!"

"Dorito hot dog?" Josh asked.

"Sure!" Cleo said.

Caylee wrinkled her nose.

"Okay," Cleo said. "Maybe not *endless*." They all laughed, but she still thought personalized lip balms had potential.

On the playground, Cleo felt like a big beach ball, full of air and enthusiasm, bounding from place to place in search of the girls whose barrettes they'd completed. They started with the sixth-graders. Each one was happy with her clips. None of them had brought money.

Caylee whispered, "Shouldn't we keep the clips until they pay?"

Cleo whispered back, "We'll bill them. Don't worry. We want girls to wear them around school today. You know, build the buzz."

"The buzz?" Caylee's forehead wrinkled.

"Yeah. *Bzzz-bzzz*." Cleo flapped her bent arms like a bee.

"What do bees have to do with selling our clips?"

"Nothing. It's business talk, Jelly. We want everyone to be buzzing like bees about our product!"

The last sixth-grader, LaLa Lopez, stuck the Yodas in her long brown hair immediately. "Wow. These are so cool. They look way better than I thought they would."

"Thanks . . . I guess?" Caylee said.

Cleo nudged Caylee. "Bzzz," she mumbled. LaLa ran off. Cleo cupped her hands around her mouth. "Don't forget to tell everyone in your class about Passion Clips!" Hopefully her satisfied customer had heard. "And you can pay us tomorrow!"

Amelie loved her microphones. But she didn't have any money.

Steffy loved her balance beams. No money.

Tessa grinned wildly when she saw her horses and Tootsie Rolls. She still had holes where her canine teeth had been, up until she'd become a client of Cleo's Quick and Painless Tooth Removal Service a couple weeks back. She loved her Passion Clips with a passion, she said. The palominos were precious. The Tootsie Rolls looked just like the real thing. And the fourteen dollars she owed them was at home.

Cleo the Beach Ball was deflated. "That's okay," she said a little glumly. "Just promise to wear them every day until you pay us. Deal?"

Tessa smiled again. "Deal!" She clipped the horses in her hair and raced off to show Steffy, who was in the field doing flips.

This time Caylee prodded Cleo. "*Bzzz-bzzz*?" She flapped her "wings."

"R-i-i-i-ght. *Bzzz-bzzz*." Cleo smiled and flapped alongside her friend. "To Principal Yu's office!" They were flitting toward the building when the whistle blew. Their delivery to the principal would have to wait.

They lined up as usual on the playground outside their classroom door. Cleo noticed that Lexie wasn't in her class line. "Where's your sister?" she asked Cole, who was just ahead of her.

"Becoming the next face of Sunshine Sparkle juice." He smirked.

"Ohhh . . . right. The commercial."

Mr. Boring opened the door and the class filed in. Cleo dangled the bags with Mr. B's orders in them. "Dolphins and books *with* your daughters' names. We hope Abigail and Alivia enjoy their Passion Clips so much they'll be begging you for more!"

Mr. B took the bags. "Thank you, girls. Make sure I give you your money before the day is over."

"Thanks, Mr. B. And don't worry. We will!" Cleo smiled at Caylee.

The morning announcements began over the

loudspeaker. Cleo snuck a peek at her teacher. He was involved in something at his desk. She held the drawstring bag down low and whispered at Cole. "Hey—will you give this to Lexie?"

Cole looked at her like, *Why should I?*

"Please?" she whispered urgently.

"I guess I can do that." He held up the sheer bag to see what was inside. "On second thought . . . no. She's already got a big enough head."

Cleo couldn't argue with that. "But you'll see her before I will." Her voice's volume rose a little too much. Mr. Boring looked up.

"*Cleo.*" He used his first finger and thumb to make a twisting motion in front of his lips. "Lock it."

Cleo clamped her mouth shut but the rest of her went into action. She pulled out a sheet of paper, folded it in thirds and ripped it along one of the creases, as quietly as she could. She wrote Lexie Lewis a bill for four dollars, including a small reminder to pay within seven days. She even included the word *please*, because she was polite as well as professional. She folded the bill, slipped it into the baggie with the clip, and wrote another note—this time to Cole. PLEASE deliver this to your sister. ☺☺☺

He read the note and wrote below it: OK. For YOU, I'll do it.

Why did he have that silly grin on his face? She ignored it and wrote one last note: THANK YOU.

Later, they were able to deliver Principal Yu his daughter's clips. He not only loved them, he promised to highlight them in the next edition of *New Heights' News*. Best of all, he had money!

At home that afternoon, Cleo hustled through her math problems, scanned her spelling words, and quickly measured each of her mealworms. "Making good progress, guys," she said into the container. "Or girls." The worms burrowed into the oat bran after their measuring ordeal.

She zoomed back to the kitchen, grabbed a pack of cheddar crackers with peanut butter, and plopped herself in front of the TV, without getting snagged by either her mom or brothers. Hallelujah! Praise the Lord!

Fortune was great, as always, but Cleo was having a hard time staying focused. When would Caylee show up with Fortune's clips? To keep herself from going bonkers, she worked on the letter she would send with the clips. During a commercial break she ran upstairs, grabbed some paper, and hurried back so she wouldn't miss anything.

Now . . . what to say? It had to be the perfect pitch. She needed not only to persuade Fortune but also to *convince* her to have Cleo on her show. She needed to tell Fortune who she was! Cleo tapped the end of her pencil on the paper.

What were her most appealing traits? Energetic. Outgoing. Persistent (of course). Adorable? Scratch that. She'd leave adorable for Lexie Lewis.

She was ambitious. Persuasive. Not afraid to take charge. Independent. But aware of the importance of being on a team. She'd been point guard in basketball the last couple of years, and she never could have won all those games without her team's much taller forwards and centers.

Last but not least, she had a great product, plenty more ideas where that one had come from, and she'd make a fantastic guest. Better than the woman who was on the show right then, demonstrating her line of cleaning supplies that used nothing but water to clean stuff.

Cleo's mind continued to wander. She imagined herself sitting next to Fortune on her studio couch, telling her about her first sale at the age of two, and how her earliest memories included watching *Fortune* with her mom, and how many businesses she'd operated since then, and how she too had big plans—to run her own corporation, to build homes in other countries for kids who had lost their parents . . .

And Cleo's birth mom would see her on the show and know it was her (because how many adopted girls in the world had been given the name Cleopatra by their birth moms?), and she'd get in touch with Fortune and Fortune would have them both on the show as a follow-up.

Cleo could picture it all. And it was perfect. She just needed to convince Fortune of the same. She started to write.

A little while later, she was crumpling her fourth piece of paper. She'd barely started this draft, but she knew it was wrong. All wrong. Getting words to sound good on paper was so much more difficult than getting them to sound good coming from her mouth.

The doorbell rang but she didn't need to get up. Josh

was already on his way to the door. A moment later, Caylee appeared in the family room. Cleo sprang to her feet. "Do you have them?"

Caylee gave her a no-teeth, *cat that's eaten the mouse* kind of smile. She nodded and reached into her craft tote. She pulled out a sheer drawstring baggie and dangled it in the air. Cleo held open her palms and Caylee gently placed the clips in her hands as if they were not merely replicas of pyramids but precious artifacts from inside an actual pharaoh's tomb.

Cleo slowly drew them from the bag.

They were *perfect*!

Caylee had sprayed the gold felt with the gold glitter paint to make the clips shimmer. She had drawn lines to make them look 3-D and to mark the levels of brick. The crowning final touch: She'd used her best cursive handwriting to write *Fortune* across the face of one pyramid and the words *Passion Is Purpose*—Fortune's Principle Number One for How to Build Your Business and Live the Life You Want—along the two sides of the other pyramid's foundation.

Cleo gave Caylee a huger-than-ever Bug-A-Hug. "I *love'em-love'em-love'em*!" She ran into the kitchen, where

Mom was working on dinner. "Mom! Look! Passion Clips for Fortune! Can we mail them tonight? Please?"

"Snazzy! Excellent work, girls." She glanced at the clock over the sink. "Post office closes in ten minutes, but I can mail them tomorrow."

Cleo groaned. "I can't wait until tomorrow!" Plus, if she left the unsealed letter with Mom, she would probably read it. If she told her mom *not* to read it, she definitely would. And she didn't want Mom to read this one. It just felt too . . . private. Which made it a risk Cleo didn't want to take.

"Do you have a padded envelope?" Cleo asked. "I want to address it myself, and . . . and decorate it in an eye-catching way! These just *have* to get through to her." She and Caylee exchanged an excited glance. "Just think, Mom! If Fortune wore our clips on air—or even had me on her show! That would be huge!"

Mom put her hand on Cleo's shoulder and looked into her face. "It would be very exciting. But, honey . . . you have to remember that Fortune Davies probably gets hundreds of messages and letters every week, many of them asking her to spotlight or promote a business or a product on her show. Don't get your hopes up too high, sweetie."

Cleo let the words slide off her like grease on a non-stick pan. She was a seed in dirt, a dog chasing a scent, a dentist with a scaler! Nothing—not even her overly cautious mom—could stop her from trying to reach Fortune.

CHAPTER 9

Best. Idea. Ever!!!

Mom drove them to school the next day so they could stop at the post office on their way. Cleo and Caylee held the padded envelope between them in front of the outgoing mail slot so Mom could take a picture with her phone.

Cleo had decorated the package with hearts, smiley faces, and stars. On the back, she'd also written two of her favorite Fortune Principles: *Surround yourself with people who believe in you* (Number Two), and *Worth is measured not by how much we earn but by how much we give* (Number

Nine), and underlined and punctuated them with lots of exclamation marks.

Mom took a picture of Cleo kissing the envelope, which Josh and Jay thought was hilarious, and another of the girls dropping it into the mail slot, their fingers crossed. Cleo said a little prayer, and it was done.

As soon as they hit the playground, it was clear: Lexie Lewis was back. She stood at the center of a crowd of girls, including most of Cleo's friends. Cleo, with Caylee in tow, strode toward the group, curious to see whether Lexie would be wearing her Passion Clip.

As they got closer, something glinted in Lexie's curly hair. The Hollywood star! She had worn it! Of course she would—after a day on the set. This was not anywhere *close* to how great it would be when Fortune wore her Passion Clips on air, but still, it was good for business.

"And we had food whenever we wanted it, *all* day long," Lexie was saying. "Sushi, designer pizzas . . ."

"Designer *pizzas*?" Mia said.

"I guess you had a good time doing the commercial," Cleo interjected.

"Not good," Lexie said. "Unbelievable!" She beamed. "It was the most incredible experience of my life!"

Cleo wanted to be happy for this girl who had had this most incredible experience. She really did. But when she thought about the mean thing Lexie had said, the hurtful words (*Why* else *would your mom give you away?*), her jaw still clenched and her chest still burned.

"Your hair looks great curly," Steffy gushed. "You should wear it that way all the time."

"The director wanted my hair like this for the shoot. She said it was the style that was most 'appealing.'"

"Your Passion Clip looks great too!" Cleo pointed out. "Yours too, Tessa." Tessa had worn her Tootsie Rolls.

"Thanks. Oh, and I have the money!" Tessa said.

Cleo felt a surge of excitement. "Great. Where is it?"

Lexie had launched back into her story.

Tessa whispered, "In my backpack. I'll get it later. I want to hear about Lexie's commercial."

Cleo looked at Caylee, ready to leave this little Lexie Lovefest, but Caylee was as transfixed as all the others. Even some boys, Micah Mitchell and Max Peacock, who had come to school with his hair dyed blue, had come over to listen.

"It was *soooo* tiring—it seemed like we had to do a hundred rehearsals and just as many takes —"

"So you made a lot of mistakes?" Cleo asked innocently.

Lexie's eyes shot poisoned darts. "No. That's just how the *professionals* do it." She turned back to the crowd. "I even had my own director's chair for the day! And my family is getting free Sunshine Sparkle for the rest of the year!" Cleo noticed she didn't try to say "fruit-flavored beverage" this time.

"I wouldn't drink that stuff if someone *paid* me to!" The very thought of the nasty gunk made Cleo's cheeks tense and her lips contort.

"Well, they paid *me* to, all right—two thousand dollars!" Lexie looked gleeful.

Even Cleo had a hard time keeping her eyes from bugging at that figure.

The group cried in amazement. "*What?*" "Wow!" "That's so much!" "I've never had that much money!"

"Can *I* be in a commercial?" Max asked, running his hand over his shock of blue hair.

Cleo wanted to ask if anyone else had remembered to bring money for the clips, but Lexie jabbered on—about how she had wowed everyone at the audition, and the cute little boy who played her brother, and how there might be a follow-up commercial if this one did well. *Yada yada yada.*

Cleo couldn't stand it anymore. Lexie wasn't the only one with exciting news. "I sent a pair of my Passion Clips to Fortune A. Davies! I'm going to get on her show!" Cleo's whole body tingled.

Everyone got dead quiet. Taylor and Mia looked at their feet. Were they trying not to laugh?

Tessa gaped. "That would be so amazing, Cleo!"

"You're joking, right?" Lexie sputtered.

Cleo felt a little sick to her stomach. She rooted herself to the ground even though everything in her wanted to flee from the circle of staring kids. "No, I'm not. It's possible. She's had kids on her show. And she's going to *love* these one-of-a-kind clips. Caylee did an awesome job."

Caylee smiled, then bit her lip and looked away.

"Let us know how that turns out," Lexie said, turning toward the building with Taylor and Mia. The whistle had blown. "And I'll give you your money at lunch—I've got plenty!"

Cleo growled.

"Forget her, Cleo. It doesn't matter." Caylee grabbed her hand and pulled her toward their classroom. "Come on."

How could Caylee say it didn't matter? Why should girls like Lexie Lewis get all the attention and the breaks?

Fortune had to like the Passion Clips. She just *had* to!

That afternoon on *Fortune*, Fortune announced something incredible. As a way to showcase kidpreneurs, she wanted kids everywhere to upload ads for the businesses they owned and operated onto her recently launched video-sharing site, FortuneTube.

Cleo couldn't believe it. This was *perfect*! And it gave Cleo the best idea she'd had in a while. In fact, this was quite possibly her *Best. Idea. Ever!!!*

The next morning, she asked Mr. Boring if all the girls could stick around for a minute before going out for recess, and he said sure. When the boys were finally gone, Cleo made her big announcement: "Everyone here is invited to a Passion Clips/Power Makeover/Ad Shoot sleepover party at my house—Friday night!"

She bounced around to each girl, handing out the invitations she'd made during "lovely language arts" when she was supposed to be working on her poem with all the similes. Mr. B surely would have stopped her had he known what she was doing, but technically she'd been writing, like everyone else. She'd been writing invitations!

"Ad shoot?" Steffy's usually flat eyebrows became little hills.

"Yes! Everyone bring your Passion Clips, or some money to buy one if you can—if you can't we'll loan you one—and we'll shoot an ad for Passion Clips to put on FortuneTube, starring . . . US!"

After she explained what FortuneTube was, most everyone seemed excited—especially Tessa, who let out a small squeal and made fast, little claps in front of her chest. Anusha was quiet, as usual. Lily, a largish girl with pale blue eyes and hair so blond it looked almost white, looked a little surprised, but then, she and Cleo had never exchanged more than a quiet hello.

Jasmine beamed. "Thanks, Cleo! I've never been to a sleepover. Unless you count cousins. And I've never *ever* been in a commercial!"

"I don't know if my parents will let me," Amelie said. "They don't know your parents."

"Mine, either," said Rosa. Her fuzzy, dark brown hair always looked as if it wanted to bust out of its braids.

"No worries. They can call and ask all the questions they want. We'll do makeovers and have an ice-cream sundae bar and there'll be lots of Passion Clips on display to give you ideas for ones you might order for yourself! Right, Caylee?"

Caylee looked like an armadillo caught in the headlights of an oncoming semitruck. "Uh . . . sure. I *guess.*"

"And then Saturday, we'll go to Wilson Park and shoot the ad!"

The girls chattered excitedly as they left the classroom for the playground.

Outside, Caylee cornered her. "I thought we were going to spend Friday night finishing the orders from your church that we still have to make. Now we'll have even more!"

"Exactly, Jelly! More orders means more money, which means the ability to make more of our product! Not to mention more clips on girls' heads is more free advertising for us. Buzz—remember? *Bzzz-bzzz?*"

"Cleo . . . I'm not sure —"

"Come on, Cay-Cay! Dream big!" Cleo swept an open hand through the air at eye level. "*Imagine*: a Passion Clip on every girl's head at New Heights Elementary."

Caylee still looked hesitant.

Cleo grabbed Caylee's arm. "Without *you*, Jelly, there's no Passion Clips!"

"But I don't know if I can make them this fast."

"You won't be making them alone. We're in this together, remember? The thing now is how to get my mom to say yes."

Caylee's eyes bugged. "You haven't asked your mom?"

"Not yet. But with my Persuasion Power at work"— she snapped her fingers—"it'll be a snap."

CHAPTER 10

Sounds like Trouble

It wasn't a snap.

"You invited nine girls to spend the night without asking first?" Hands on hips. Uh-oh. That was Mom Sign Language for "I am thoroughly exasperated with you and most likely will say no even if what you want is totally doable."

They were in the kitchen. Cleo dug through the snack cabinet. Why wasn't there ever anything *good*?

"Cleo?"

"What? We've got a whole two days to prepare." She

shoved her hand into a box of crackers and started to chow down. "And it's not just a sleepover. It's a Passion Clips/Power Makeover/Ad Shoot party."

Mom huffed. "Party. Sleepover. It doesn't matter. And it's not about being prepared. You need to get our permission before you make plans! Did you wash your hands?"

Cleo slumped but she put the box down. She went to the sink and washed.

"How many times do we have to go over this? Remember, the whole 'board of directors' thing? You're supposed to come to us first with all your great ideas."

"That was for all my great *business* ideas."

"Yes . . . but we're your parents. You run ideas and plans—of *any* kind—by us first! And, anyway, you said it yourself—this party is for your business."

"True. I am hoping to sell some clips, and we *are* going to make a video for Fortune's website. But, Mom, you don't have to worry. I've got it all worked out." She snatched up the box and resumed snacking. "We'll sleep on the floor in the family room. There's space. We can order pizza, and we're going to do power makeovers like on *Fortune* —"

"Ordering pizza is expensive, Cleo." Mom's lips were tensed. The lines between her eyebrows were deep.

"I invited Mia." She'd decided to include Mia, even though she wasn't in her class this year. Caylee, Tessa, Steffy, Cleo, and Mia had all been in Ms. Nuesmeyer's for fourth grade. "You're always asking if I want to get together with Mia." Mia was the other African-American girl in her circle of school friends. "Well, here's a great chance!"

Mom's jaw softened. She closed her eyes, took a breath. Opened her eyes again. "Okay."

Cleo jumped. "Thanks, Mom!"

"Not 'okay' we'll do it. 'Okay,' we'll talk about it later, after your dad gets home. Right now, you need to do your homework."

Cleo started to groan, but Mom gave her a look. "You don't have any room to complain, missy. You've just asked for something *big*. It would be in your best interest to cooperate."

"But I need to go to Caylee's house so we can make more clips!"

"Finish your homework, and you can."

Mom had made her conditions clear. Time to let it go . . . for now.

In her room, she measured each of her corporate executive mealworms—super challenging on account of how much they wriggled. She had to hold them flat, hoping she wasn't squishing them. Next, she raced them in heats of two to see who was fastest (one of her questions) and recorded the results in her notebook.

She sat at her desk, daydreaming about the sleepover. What would it be like to have nine girls at her house? She'd have to make sure her brothers were on their best behavior. She'd bribe them—a DinoFormer for each of them if they stayed out of the way all night.

Mom called at her door. "How's it going, Cleo?"

"Fine!" she called back. She opened her backpack and got out the book she'd checked out for her first book report. Ms. Tomasello, the librarian, had recommended the novel: *The Great Gilly Hopkins*. Cleo got settled on her bed and opened to where she'd left off. Gilly was explaining her name. Her mother (who had left and didn't seem to be coming back) had named her after a powerful queen named Galadriel.

Cleo's heart got pricked reading that. *Her* mother had named her after a powerful queen. Her mother had left, and didn't seem to be coming back. Maybe she *wouldn't* do her report on Gilly Hopkins. The girl may have been great, but Cleo wasn't convinced reading about her would be.

She glanced at the closet, where she kept the flat gift

box that held the only things she had from her birth mom, other than Beary, her stuffed purple bear. A heart necklace, small heart earrings, a baby outfit covered with orange butterflies, and the photo of Cleo as a brand-new baby in her birth mom's brown arms. Beary was in the picture too—stuffed between the hospital bed railing and her birth mom's hip.

Cleo dropped the book on the bed and picked up Beary. She pressed her cheek against the top of the bear's well-worn head. When she was younger—five or six, like Josh—she would lie in bed and rub Beary like a genie's lamp, wishing over and over that her birth mom might suddenly reappear and be there again as she was in that photograph, her arms around Cleo.

She hugged Beary harder. She was ten. Old enough to know better. Her birth mom wasn't coming back. Her fingers circle-stroked the soft purple fur, in spite of what she told herself.

Please come back. I love my mom, but I need you too.

A cacophony of voices, squeals, and barking brought her back to reality. Dad was home. She propped Beary against her pillow, giving the stuffed animal one last, lingering look.

"Mail call!" Dad shouted from the living room.

Cleo took the stairs two at a time. There could be a letter from Fortune!

"Anything for me?" Josh said over and over.

"Meeeee!!!" JayJay screeched.

"As a matter of fact, there is." He pulled a padded envelope from the stack. "Something from your first mom."

Melanie, the boys' birth mom, mostly lived in central California. She had some kind of imbalance in her brain (although Cleo thought she seemed friendly enough), which is why Josh and Jay had ended up in foster care, and then, eventually, getting adopted by Cleo and her parents.

Josh grabbed the envelope and tore into it hungrily.

"Mine too!" JayJay cried, tugging on the package.

The envelope went flying. Cleo spied Melanie's slanted, loopy cursive. Josh started to whale on JayJay.

"Whoa. Whoa!" Dad got a hand on each of them and pulled them apart. Mom grabbed JayJay. Dad held Josh. "Boys, that's not how we treat each other. Time to cool off." He directed them to opposite corners of the room.

Cleo picked up the package.

"That's mine! She can't open it!" Josh yelled.

"Sometimes she sends me things too," Cleo said innocently.

"Cleo," Mom said firmly. "Is your name on the envelope?"

Cleo looked, then shook her head. "Is there any mail for me?" A slightly hurt tone tinged her voice.

Dad looked through the rest of the pile. "Sorry, Sunshine. Not today."

Mom held her hand toward Cleo. "Bring it to me, please."

Cleo gripped the package. She had the urge to run upstairs and hide it from all of them. Why did her brothers have to get a present from their birth mom on that particular afternoon? It felt especially unfair.

She handed over the package, then plopped in a chair at the dining table. She started to bring up the sleepover, but Mom shook her head, her finger pressed against her mouth. "Not a good time, Cleo."

When the boys were calm again, Mom brought JayJay to her lap. She patted the couch next to her. "Come on over, Josh." Cleo plopped her chin onto her hand. They were all in the same room, but she felt far away, as if she were watching her family on television or from outer space.

"You each get to take a turn. Pull one thing out at a time," Mom directed. "Jay first."

Josh started to protest, but Mom cut him off. "You'll each get the same number of turns."

Jay reached in and pulled out a Hot Wheels. "Yay!" he shouted.

Josh pulled out a yo-yo and wrinkled his nose.

"What?" Dad said. "Yo-yos are totally cool! You can do tricks, like 'walk the dog' . . ."

Barkley barked and then whined, looking at his leash hanging by the door. That got everyone to smile, even Cleo. "In a little while, buddy," Dad said, laughing.

The boys each pulled out bouncy rubber balls and slingshots (which Mom wasn't too pleased about), another Hot Wheels for Josh and a yo-yo for Jay.

Josh turned the envelope upside down. A card fluttered out. Mom picked it up, while Josh got down on the floor and sent his Hot Wheels car careening across the floorboards.

Mom read the note from Melanie. "For my boys . . . to celebrate a new school year."

Cleo crossed her arms. "How is that a special occasion?" she scoffed. "Jay doesn't even go to real school."

"Yes, I do!" Jay protested. "I go to school two days a week."

"Cleo . . ." Mom warned.

"Whatever," Cleo mumbled. "She's not my mom, anyway. She's *theirs*." As soon as it was out of her mouth, Cleo regretted it, because she said it out of her hurt and because it wasn't the whole truth. *Mom* was the boys' mom now, because of the adoption. But they had another mom too, just as Cleo did. She just didn't know where hers was.

"Hey, guys," Dad broke the silence. "Why don't you take your new toys outside, and I'll come teach you some cool yo-yo tricks in a bit."

"Okay!" They scooped up their spoils and headed for the back door. Barkley trotted after them.

"Stay inside the fence," Mom reminded them. Julian, in particular, had been known to venture out. Pedro and Fred down the street had returned him safely more than once.

Julian stopped before reaching the kitchen. He came back to Cleo, holding out his plastic blue yo-yo. "This is for you, Cleo." His face was serious, his chin held high.

"No, JayJay. It's okay. Melanie meant for you to have it."

He pressed the yo-yo into her chest, right over her heart.

"She made a mistake," he said matter-of-factly. His brown eyes were determined.

Cleo took the yo-yo. She wrapped her arm around his neck, pulling him close. "Thanks, JayJay. You're a really good brother." He dashed from the room. Cleo looked up at her parents. They didn't say anything, and neither did Cleo. But she smiled, and things felt a little closer to normal.

"So . . ." Mom said. "You want to have a sleepover. This Friday night."

Cleo grinned and rushed to the couch. She was suddenly energized, like a stockbroker being told to buy. "Can I? Dad?" Mom pulled on her arm and she landed in Dad's lap. "And it's not just a sleepover. It's a —"

"*Passion Clips/Power Makeover/Ad Shoot party*. I know, I know." Mom turned to Dad. "What do you think, Charlie? You all right with ten girls taking over our family room for the night?"

Dad's eyes opened wide. "*Ten?* Sounds like trouble to me."

"We won't be. I promise! We'll be perfect!" Cleo looked straight into his eyes.

He smiled. "I don't need perfect. Just considerate. But there's one condition."

"Anything!" Cleo said, bouncing a little on his lap.

"You absolutely can *not* have any fun."

She bopped him on the chest. "Da-ad!"

"Okay," Mom said, taking a deep breath. "I guess we're doing it."

Cleo threw her arms in the air and cheered. "Thank you! We're going to do our hair, and maybe . . . makeup?" She batted her eyelashes at Mom.

"Don't push it, kid."

"Okay, okay," Cleo rushed on. "And order pizza, and make a very persuasive ad for Passion Clips!" She paused. "I'm sorry I didn't ask before inviting friends over."

"*Nine* friends." Mom fixed one squinty eye on Cleo.

"What can I say? I think big!"

Mom's eyes turned smiley. "Apology accepted."

"At least I didn't invite any boys."

"Are you sure?" Dad dug his fingers into her ribs. "Because if any show up, I'll have to run them off."

She laughed and squirmed off his lap, into the space between her parents. "I'm sure! Boys aren't my key demographic."

Mom's eyebrows popped up. "Your key demographic?"

"Yeah, you know, my primary customers. Except Micah Mitchell. He wants a pair."

Mom put her arm around Cleo. "You're amazing. How do you know so much about these things—business and selling? And *demographics*, for heaven's sake!"

They all said the answer together: "Fortune, of course!"

Cleo pressed her knees together, kept her eyes on her clasped hands. "My birth parents could be business-people. Maybe I got it from one of them."

"It's possible," Dad said. "I read recently that scientists think they've discovered a risk-taking gene."

"That's not one I got," Mom said. That was for sure. Mom was always telling Cleo and her brothers to be care-ful. To stay inside the fence.

"You have to take risks in the world of business," Cleo reminded her parents.

"So I've heard," Dad said. "Well-calculated, but risks, nonetheless."

Cleo sensed the risk of her next question, but she had to know. "Couldn't we try to find out more about *my* birth par-ents? Like their names or where they live?" Had she felt her mom stiffen beside her? Cleo couldn't look her in the face.

"Well . . . it's tricky, honey," Mom replied. "That infor-mation isn't available to us."

"But Josh and Jay know *Melanie.* They even get presents from her! And I know nothing." She had almost added, "I get nothing," but the blue yo-yo in her hands stopped her. "All I have is Beary and those few things from when I was a baby. It's not fair!"

Mom sighed. "Oh, honey. I would have loved for you to know your birth parents, but that's not the way they chose to do it."

"But *why?*" Cleo searched Mom's face for an answer, but it wasn't there.

"I don't know." Her eyes were sad.

Cleo looked back into her lap. "She's probably a homeless person. A crazy homeless person. Who lives in her car." In her mind, she added, *I could have lived in her car with her.*

Dad put his hand on her arm. "Whoa, now. We've told you, remember? Your birth mom was a young college student. She wasn't married to your birth dad. She did what she thought was best." Dad took her chin in his hand. His round eyes were kind. "I have no doubt, my Sunshine, no doubt —" his voice broke. Was Dad about to cry? "It caused her a world of hurt to part with you."

Cleo nodded, but she didn't really understand. Why did people do the things they did? Mom had said something the other day . . . *We all do things that aren't good for us.* Had adoption been good or bad for her? For her birth mom? And what about her birth dad? Where was he?

She had to admit she was glad she didn't live in a car. But if her birth mom had been a college student, they could have done all right. Couldn't they have?

CHAPTER 11

Picture Day

Thursday morning (picture day!), Cleo was up early to take out the curlers and twists the stylist had put in the night before at Salon Go Natural, the place Mom took Cleo to for occasional conditioning treatments, trims, and in this case, the twist-n-curl style that Cleo loved. One, it was more mature-looking than braids, and two, it was how Fortune wore her hair!

Cleo practiced her smile in the bathroom mirror. Outside of the last day of school, picture day was her favorite day of the year.

She made eyes at herself, trying out different expressions. Could she look as radiant and successful as Fortune did in her poster? She raised her eyebrows, opened her eyes wider, showed more teeth, less teeth, no teeth. More teeth made her look like she'd eaten one two many Kit Kats; less teeth made her look like her pants were too tight; no teeth made her look as if she were plotting world domination. Nothing made her look as carefree and confident as Fortune.

Mom knocked. "Ready to unveil those gorgeous locks?"

Cleo cracked the door. "I guess."

"What's up? You've been begging me for a twist-n-curl since school started."

Cleo shrugged. She slumped on the toilet lid. Mom unsnapped the perm rods at the ends of Cleo's twists and gently unrolled them one at a time. The lines between Mom's eyebrows made her look mad, but the way she was holding her tongue between her teeth told Cleo she was just concentrating.

At the salon, Cleo had thought that if her birth mom were her mom, they'd be sitting side by side getting their hair done, instead of her mom sitting in the waiting area reading a magazine. "I wish we had the same hair," she said.

"That'd be kind of awkward, wouldn't it? We'd have to take turns wearing it."

Cleo scowled. *"Mom."*

"I'm sorry. Bad one." She started to undo the twists. "Why do you wish we had the same type of hair?"

"It would just be easier. Don't you think?"

"Easier in what way?"

"Well . . ." Cleo wasn't sure how to put into words what she was feeling. "We could get our hair done at the same place, instead of you going to that other salon." That wasn't even her biggest concern, but she didn't know how, or whether, to say what was.

"Ah, yes . . . Ruby-Do's. They're pros with boring, straight hair like mine." She looked in the mirror and fluffed her short, brown "practical mom bob," as she called it. She finished undoing the last twist in Cleo's hair, then put her fingers deep into Cleo's thick mane and scratched at her roots to loosen everything up. "You know, I never really thought about it, but now that you bring it up, maybe I *can* get my hair done at Salon Go Natural."

"Do they do hair like yours?"

"I don't know, but I'm going to ask Miss Merlean. It sure is kind of her to display Passion Clips at her front desk."

Cleo got as perky as her new hairdo. "I *know*! We'll get more orders for sure. Miss Merlean's almost as much of a salesperson as I am!"

Mom laughed and then stepped back so Cleo could look in the mirror.

Cleo saw and felt the real smile that beamed from her face. She shook her head, enjoying the feel of her springy curls bouncing against one another. She stood still again as Mom finished off the ends by wrapping them one section at a time around her finger to smooth the ringlets. Mom may not have had the same hair as Cleo, but she worked hard to help Cleo with the hair she had—thick, coily-curly, and with a mind of its own, just like Cleo. And Cleo loved her mom for it. But she still wished Mom had hair that was more like hers.

"Will you send my school picture to the agency again?" Cleo asked. In her head, she added, *Just in case . . .*

"Of course. And an update. Like I do every year."

Cleo knew the picture and letter weren't really for the adoption agency. They were for her birth parents. In case they ever wanted to know how Cleo was doing. Cleo stuffed the thought that one of them might see the pictures and letters and get in touch. Why would this year be any different than others?

School went quickly. Picture day helped. Cleo's class spent more than a half hour in the multipurpose room getting their photos taken. When it was her turn in front of the camera, Cleo flashed her biggest, brightest CEO smile ever. She was confident this year's picture would be her best one yet. She was the president of her own company, and her and Caylee's current product was a stunning success! Nothing could stop her now!

When Cleo got home that afternoon, Mom had out her fancy Global Chef!® knife and was chopping like a maniac.

"What are those?" Cleo asked, looking at the plump, brown, dried-fruit-like things on Mom's cutting board. "They look like mealworms that've been fed too many Kit Kats. *If* they ate chocolate, that is. Which they don't— crazy worms."

"They're dates. For Cleo's Canine Cookies." Mom kept chopping. "I'm aiming for a product launch in three weeks."

Cleo grinned. "Really? At the farmers' market?"
Mom nodded.

"That's great! Can I help you sell them?"

"*Can* you?" She swiped the dates into a bowl. "I'm counting on it!"

The boys came running in. "We're hungry!" Jay yelled.

"Can we have something to eat?" Josh asked.

Mom asked Cleo to get out what they needed to make ants-on-a-boat: apples, peanut butter, and raisins. While Cleo did that, she told them all about picture day, including how Micah Mitchell was entertaining everyone in line with his talking kneecaps.

"How do kneecaps talk?" Josh wanted to know.

Cleo pulled up her pants above her knee and pinched her loose knee skin so that it looked like a pair of lips. She pushed on the folded skin so that the lips "moved." "Hello! I'm a talking kneecap," she said in a silly voice.

Josh and Jay giggled. Immediately, they made their kneecaps start talking to each other.

"Micah calls his kneecaps Ron and Hermione."

"He sounds like a creative kid," Mom said, spreading peanut butter on an apple quarter. Cleo topped that with a row of raisins.

"Micah? He's unique, all right. But I like him. I might

even recruit him to work for Cleopatra Enterprises— product development, perhaps. I've been thinking we should do more to tap into the boy market."

Mom put the finished apples on a plate. "To the table, please."

Cleo took the ants-on-a-boat to the other room. She felt like she could eat a real boat she was so ravenous.

Barkley sniffed around the edge of the table. Jay scooped peanut butter from one of his apples and let Barkley lick his fingers.

"Jay! Don't feed the dog peanut butter," Mom said, coming into the room. "He's still on a diet."

Barkley's tongue had gone into overdrive trying to get the sticky stuff off the roof of his mouth.

"Plus it's cruel." Mom shook her head, but the rest of them snickered watching Barkley smack his lips.

Cleo bit into the crunchy-gooey-sweet-salty snack.

"Hey, speaking of Cleopatra Enterprises," said Mom, "I've got some good news for you."

Cleo dropped her apple. "Why didn't you tell me?"

"I'm telling you."

"What is it?" Cleo looked around for a pile of mail. "Did Fortune write back?"

"Sorry, hon. Not that. But it *is* a promotional opportunity." Her eyebrows lifted. "Nationwide." Her face wore a satisfied smile.

"*What!* Mom, what is it? You have to tell me right now!"

The back door opened and shut. "Anyone home?" Dad called.

The boys zoomed from the table, shouting, "Dad! Dad!" A moment later, Dad appeared, one son hanging from either arm. "Soc-cer! Soc-cer!" Josh shouted. Jay joined in the chant.

"Stop yelling!" Cleo yelled.

The boys stopped and stared.

"Can you please just get to my good news?"

Mom and Dad exchanged a look.

"Go warm up your kicking feet, boys," Dad said. "I'll be out in a few."

Josh grabbed his Dodgers cap (he never went outside without it) and made a break for the front door.

"Wait for me!" Jay yelled. Barkley loped after them in a hurry not to get trapped inside.

"As you were saying . . ." Cleo looked expectantly at Mom. Dad pulled up a chair. Something in Mom's eyes had changed. She seemed a little less happy, as if a small amount of a different hue had gotten stirred in and changed the color of her expression.

"Something about a promotional opportunity?" Cleo prompted.

"Right. The promotional opportunity." Mom put on her business face. Cleo liked when they talked this way. "Well . . . I spoke with the adoption agency today. I told them about what you've been up to . . . that you've had a string of businesses, which you're now calling Cleopatra Enterprises, and about your latest business and how it's really taking off."

"And . . . ?"

"Of course they loved that you and Caylee are donating a portion of your profits to help orphans attend school."

"*Mom!*" Cleo couldn't wait any longer.

"They want to do a feature article in their national magazine—online and in print! Isn't that wonderful?"

"Wow! That's fantastic! Thanks, Mom."

"And, there's something else." Mom took a sip of air. "It may be kind of surprising at first."

Cleo's heart was thumping. Why was she suddenly nervous?

"It's sort of crazy . . . the timing of it all . . . but I say I believe in divine intervention, so this must all be part of God's plan."

Dad rested his hand on Mom's fidgeting ones.

Cleo's heart surged. She felt a little sick to her stomach. "You asked about my birth parents. They're dead, aren't they?" It was something she often thought but had never said out loud.

Mom looked shocked. "Oh. No. I don't think . . . well, your birth father for sure isn't." The space between her eyebrows wrinkled. She looked to Dad. "Charlie?"

Her birth *father*? Cleo hardly ever thought about her birth dad—not nearly as much as her birth mom. And how did Mom know he wasn't dead, anyway? What had she found out? And what about her birth mother?

"Your birth father," Dad said, "lives in West LA." He looked Cleo straight in the eyes. "And he would like to meet you. If you want."

Cleo's head was spinning. If she wanted . . . she could meet . . . her *birth father*?

"What about my birth mom?" Her words felt sticky on her tongue.

Mom's lips tightened. Her wrinkles stood out like parentheses around her mouth. She shook her head.

"But he could tell me about her, right?"

"Possibly. But we need to take this one step at a time, Cleo. First, we need to talk about whether you want to meet him."

Cleo had a terrible thought. What if he wasn't the right one? How did they know he was her birth father? How did *he* know he was her birth father? What if someone had made a mistake? What if he was only pretending to be her birth father for some reason?

"Cleo?" Mom's hand was on her arm.

"How do they know it's really him?"

"They know his name. And other information about him."

"They do?" Cleo felt confused. "How come they knew but we didn't?"

Mom took a deep breath. "It happens sometimes that the birth parents prefer not to share that information with the child or the new family. We've talked about this, honey."

It was true, they had. She'd just never put it together that the agency had this information. Had *always* had this information. While she hadn't.

"But how come we can know about him now but we couldn't before?" This was all very confusing.

"Apparently, he contacted the agency and let them know he was open to us getting in touch with him," Dad said, "a while ago. But someone made a mistake and the message never got passed along."

"A mistake?" She felt a surge of anger and then light-headedness. Her fingertips tingled.

"Your mom and I were always open to having a relationship with your birth parents, like we do with Melanie. So —"

"You're still our daughter," Mom cut in. "That will never change." She looked at Cleo intently. This was the face that had drawn near to kiss Cleo almost every day of her life. Round and pale, like the moon. Blue eyes, freck-led cheeks, short nose. The only face Cleo had ever known as "mom."

She looked at Dad. Brown eyes, square jaw, long nose, olive skin. The only face she had ever known as "dad."

"What's his name?" she asked.

"Kelvin," Dad said. "Kelvin Banks."

She thought about that for a moment. So she could have been Cleopatra Banks? Wow. It had a nice ring.

She nodded, squinting. Still thinking. "I like Cleopatra Edison Oliver better."

Mom's eyes brightened but neither of her parents spoke. They watched her, waiting.

"Do you think I should meet him?"

"We think it's up to you," Dad said. "And you can take as much time as you want to decide."

Caylee's dad had left; his pictures were gone. Cleo's dad had suddenly shown up, on picture day. How strange. The weight of it pressed down on her, making it difficult to take in.

A birth dad could tell her about birth grandparents and birth aunts and uncles and cousins. Most important, he could tell her about her birth mom. She could have a birth-relatives list—like Caylee. It was what she had been wanting.

Why then was she feeling so unsure?

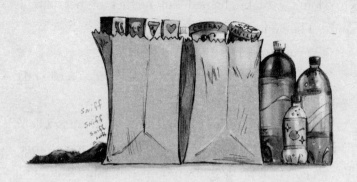

CHAPTER 12

Last-Minute Jitters

That night, Cleo insisted on going shopping with Mom for the Passion Clips party. She wanted to make sure Mom didn't come home with only healthy stuff to put on the sundaes. As for meeting her birth dad, she had told her parents she couldn't make a decision about that. Not until after the party, at least.

Cleo and Mom got in the minivan and headed to WinCo, the huge chain store that had moved in and put Grandpa Williams's little corner grocery out of business. Cleo normally refused to step foot in the mega-store, out of loyalty to him. Her own large corporation, once she had one, would be a socially conscious company that paid attention to its impact on the local community.

Mom had her principles too, but when it came to groceries—especially buying a bunch of food for a party she hadn't planned—it had to be as economical as possible. Cleo was in no position to persuade otherwise.

At WinCo, they *did* get healthy berries, but they also got whipped cream and hot fudge. They skipped peanuts, in case anyone was allergic, but got maraschino cherries because, as Cleo argued, they could also be put in Shirley Temples. Cleo picked out three half gallons of ice cream and six take-n-bake pizzas. When she couldn't decide between a second two-liter of root beer (her favorite) or a first two-liter of Coke, Mom told her to go ahead and get both, in addition to the Strawberry Crush and Sprite already in the cart.

Cleo threw her arms around Mom's neck and kissed her cheek. "Thanks for letting me do this party, Mom!" She knew her mom could have so easily squashed the whole un-preapproved plan.

A white woman farther down the soda-snack aisle watched them.

"I'm glad that you want your friends to come over to our house," Mom said, pushing the cart forward.

"Hopefully you'll still feel that way Saturday afternoon!" They laughed loudly.

The woman stared on. Did she think they were being too noisy? Or was it something else? On one hand, Cleo was used to the gazes. On the other, most people at least *tried* to look as if they weren't looking.

When Cleo was younger, Mom (or Dad) would sometimes say to a stranger at a restaurant or a playground something like, "My daughter is beautiful, isn't she?" and Cleo would feel proud and special. As she got older, she realized they were saying it to *staring* strangers, and she stopped liking it so much. She told her parents she didn't want them saying anything anymore.

The lady went back to her shopping as Cleo and her mom pushed past her and around the corner.

"I wanted so badly to say something," Mom said, "but I knew you wouldn't appreciate it."

"You were right."

Mom squeezed her hand.

At the checkout, Cleo's eyes bugged at the grand total: $112! For *one* sleepover. That her parents hadn't planned to have.

"We can put the extra root beer back." Cleo reached for the bag with the sodas. "And the cherries."

Mom stopped her. "We didn't go over budget by too much. Plus, Dad said he's getting his extra check soon for coaching." She looked Cleo straight on. "Just enjoy the party, okay?"

Cleo nodded. She could do that.

At school the next day, Cleo couldn't stop watching the clock, which meant the day went even slower than usual. A couple of times she started to say something to Caylee about her birth dad showing up, but it just felt too private, even for her best friend. She also wasn't sure it was actually happening, and she didn't want to say it was happening if it wasn't. That would just hurt too badly.

The Passion Clips party going perfectly—that could be her only focus. She would tell Caylee about the other stuff after the sleepover.

When Mr. Boring finally let them pack their things at the end of the day, Cleo was first to the door. "Mr. B, can the girls be at the front of the line today? We're having a sleepover at my house!" She wanted to gather her guests one last time to make sure everyone had all the details.

"All of you?"

"Yep."

"Wow. What's the special occasion? Birthday?"

"Not until January. And the special occasion is Passion Clips, of course! Speaking of which, I hope your daughters love theirs."

"They sure do." Mr. Boring stood at the head of the line. "Men, ladies first today." The boys grumbled in protest as the girls surged forward.

"How come I wasn't invited?" Cole said in a smart-alecky voice.

Cleo crossed her arms. "Three words: Be. Oh. Why."

The bell rang and Mr. Boring opened the door. "Have a great weekend, everyone!"

Cleo talked to the girls as they exited the room in a small herd. "Six o'clock. Bring your hair things and a cute outfit for the shoot tomorrow . . . and money for clips! And don't forget my address: 818 Camphor Street! See you then!"

Ms. Sanchez's class streamed from the neighboring door. Cleo hoped Mia would be alone, or at least not with

Lexie Lewis. As soon as Mia appeared, Cleo ran over. "See you tonight at six?"

"I might be a little late, depending on when my parents pick me up." Mia went to Ms. Marti's Martial Arts every day after school, since her parents worked. Caylee joined them as they walked toward the front, where Ms. Marti's van picked up kids and Josh would be standing outside his classroom, waiting.

"Will you be my other makeover stylist?" Cleo asked. "And can you bring your flat iron?"

"Sure." Mia looked as if she had something else to say, but wasn't sure she should say it.

"Your parents said it was okay for you to be in the video?"

"Yeah, it's fine." She glanced at Cleo, still walking. "I think Lexie's upset that she wasn't invited."

Cleo scoffed. "Lexie Lewis? She doesn't even like me!"

"I'm just telling you what it seems like to me. I probably shouldn't have said anything." Mia started talking even faster than usual. "I gotta run. Ms. Marti won't wait around forever, and if I miss the van my parents *won't* let me come. I'll be grounded. See you later!"

"That's crazy," Cleo said to Caylee. "Why would Lexie even care?"

Caylee shrugged. "Maybe she just feels left out."

Cleo huffed. "Or maybe she just can't stand not being at the center of the universe."

Josh stood against the wall, alone. His hair stuck out from under his Dodgers cap. He stalked toward Cleo. "What took you so long? I'm growing old here." He hitched up his backpack. They headed for home.

They split up at Cleo's house. Caylee said she'd come back as soon as she had her overnight things.

"Don't forget the Passion Clips!" Cleo called after her.

"How could I?" Caylee said, grinning.

This was going to be so much fun! Cleo thought. And then she saw her front yard, which suddenly seemed not very well-kept, with weeds here and there and patches of dirt where Barkley had dug up the grass or the boys had worn it away with their running around. Caylee's grass was lush and green, with perfectly kept edges. Caylee's flower beds were full of *flowers*, not weeds—blooms of fuchsia, yellow, and white. Roses that grew on lattices (a word she only knew because of Caylee's mom).

Why weren't they having their Passion Clips party at Caylee's glorious, gigantic pink villa? If only she'd thought first and planned ahead better, they could have. Instead, all the girls in her class (plus Mia) would come here and see her torn-up yard and the baby-poop-brown stucco hacienda standing before her, which was small, cramped, cluttered, and came with two little brothers!

Maybe it wasn't too late. She rushed inside and grabbed the phone off its cradle. Caylee answered. "Jelly! Change of plans! Can we have the party at your place?"

"Uh . . . I don't think my mom is going to be here."

Mom came into the living room with her hands raised in a questioning position and a *What are you talking about?* look on her face.

Cleo sighed. "Never mind. It's okay. See you in a few." She quietly put the phone back. She sat on the couch circling her wrist, listening for the click in the joint. Seven in a row was good luck.

Mom sat next to her. "What's going on?"

"Our yard! It looks so junky! And our house—it's too small, and messy, and . . . and what was I *thinking* inviting all these girls over?" she wailed. She put her hands over her face.

"Cleo, it's going to be fine. You're just having a case of last-minute jitters. We've still got a little over two hours. So, what can we do to get ready?"

Cleo put her hands on her legs and looked around. Mom was right. She needed to take action, not freak out. She'd been giving in to wishful thinking, something Fortune preached never to do. As Fortune always said, "You can whine or you can win. You can complain or you can commit. You can moan or you can move. What are you going to do?" What could she do to impress her guests from the moment they stepped out of their parents' cars?

A sign. In the window. WELCOME, GUESTS, it would read. Honored Guests? Esteemed Guests? No. *Passion Clip Partiers!*

Yes!

She took a deep breath. "Okay. You're right. I got this, Mom."

Mom slapped Cleo's leg. "That's my girl. Go get 'em."

Cleo got out her sign-making materials and was making her first sign when Caylee arrived. Together they finished it and hung it in the window. This was great! The sign would not only welcome her guests, it would give their product more exposure among her neighbors. In fact, this weekend she would go door-to-door. Ms. Chu might have a niece or granddaughter out there somewhere. And Cleo could easily persuade Fred and Pedro to buy one for Bowmore. The terrier's hair was always getting in his eyes.

She and Caylee got out crepe paper and balloons left-over from JayJay's birthday in June and hung the stuff everywhere—around the sign, from the porch light, around the pillars on the front porch. She didn't have time to grow new grass or weed the flower beds, but she *could* divert people's attention to something else. Something fun and party-like!

Her brothers came out and begged for balloons. Jay, wearing a too-big pair of Josh's hand-me-downs, had to keep hitching up his pants as he bounced around.

She blew up two balloons and told them to play keep-away from Barkley in the driveway. They sped off toward the back of the house. Hopefully Mom had a plan for keeping the boys out of her and her guests' hair later. After all, their hair would be busy getting styled!

They decorated the chain-metal fence by weaving crepe paper through the links all the way around and tying balloons in every color of the rainbow every few feet. The balloons bobbed and danced in the late-September breeze.

Cleo stood back and took it all in. Voilà! Her house looked well-loved instead of worn-down, festive instead of falling apart.

Back inside, she and Caylee set up the family room for power makeovers. They hung another sign they'd made— SALON PERFECTO—on the wall outside the entrance. They brought in two dining chairs to be the salon chairs. Cleo raided her and Mom's bathroom drawers for the tools that would transform them from regular fifth-graders into fabulous fashionistas, each one sporting her unique, personalized Passion Clips.

"I just had a splendarvelous idea!" she said as they lined up combs, brushes, and hair accessories on the coffee table in front of the chairs. "I'll ask my dad to do 'before' and 'after' shots that we can email to everyone."

"That's great!" Caylee said, setting up a Passion Clips display on the end table next to the love seat.

It *was* great. Everything was great. Persuasion Power had worked again. This time on herself!

CHAPTER 13

A Different Kind of Superpower

"I know I said no to makeup, but how about this glitter powder I found in the back of my closet?" Mom handed Cleo a gold-lidded container and a makeup brush. "For a little extra bling."

Cleo snatched the powder, grinning. "Thanks, Mom! We can definitely use that." The doorbell rang, revving up Cleo's motor. "It's go time, people!" She zoomed from the room, praying her brothers hadn't embarrassed her already. Knowing them, they'd be rolling around on top of each other all over the patchy "yard."

She opened the door to Tessa and her dad. He had the same big front teeth and overbite as his daughter. "Hi, Tess —" Cleo looked past Tessa to see all the balloons except one lone red one flopping against the fence like tattered rags. *Popped!*

Cleo came onto the front porch. "Josh! Julian! You are *so* in trouble!"

"Everything okay?" Tessa's dad asked. "Is your mom here?" He put his hands on Tessa's shoulders.

"I'm here!" Mom called, coming through the living room. She and Mr. Hutchfield shook hands and started their adult chitchat. Cleo fumed, considering whether to hunt her brothers down immediately or exact vengeance later. *The little vandals.*

"I like the sign in your window," Tessa said, then pointed to her horse clips. "I'm ready to party!"

Cleo looked at her friend. "What? Oh! Us too. I mean, Caylee and me. She helped with the sign. And the" — she looked around the yard. The last word came out flat — "decorations."

Tessa looked at her sympathetically. Her dad gave her a kiss on the forehead, said he'd see her the next day, and left.

"Cleo, why don't you show Tessa where to put her things?" Mom said.

Cleo pointed to the fence instead. "Mom, look! The balloons!"

Mom invited Tessa to go through to the back, then spoke to Cleo alone. "I'll watch the boys, you take care of your guests."

"But they vandalized my decorations!"

"Did you see them do it?"

Cleo crossed her arms.

Mom raised her eyebrows. "Cleo?"

Cleo huffed. "No. But who else would have done it?"

"Around here, it's innocent until *proven* guilty. I'll get out the snacks. You welcome your friends."

Cleo wanted to find her brothers and extract a confession but girls started showing up with their parents. She stayed by the door and Caylee took them to the family room to stow their things and show them her latest Passion Clip creations. Mom had put out snacks—and not just a veggie tray!—to tide them over until dinner. Everything was back on track.

When there was a lull in the arrivals, Cleo realized she should take down the raggedy balloons while she had a chance. Just then, Barkley came bounding around the corner of the house. He shot like an arrow (a fat and not-too-quick arrow) headed for the bull's-eye of the red balloon. The boys chased after him, shouting.

Amelie, the girl whose family spent every summer in France, was walking up with her mom as Jay tackled Barkley. The dog dragged him across the yard, taking more grass out with him. Josh grabbed Barkley's collar. "No, Barkley!" Barkley hacked and wheezed but kept lunging forward.

Mia and her mom came up behind Amelie. They all stood frozen on the walkway, probably wondering if it was safe to come any closer.

Jay was still being dragged across the ground, his pants getting dangerously low. Cleo watched, horrified. All the girls had come onto the front porch. They stood gawking.

"Couldn't you keep them inside?" Cleo whispered to Caylee.

"No one was talking. It was getting *awkward*."

This was getting awkward.

"Let go, Josh!" Mom yelled. Josh did, but Jay held on.

Barkley made one last straining effort, snatching the red balloon in his mouth. The balloon popped, and Jay lost his pants. All the way down to his ankles. At least his underwear hadn't gone with them.

Cleo smacked her forehead with her palm. Her guests giggled. "This party's starting off with a bang," Mia joked. Mia's mom laughed—the same high-pitched tinkling as Mia.

Barkley lay on the ground chewing what was left of the balloon.

"Sorry, Cleo," Josh said. "We tried to keep him away from them, but he popped them all."

Mom raised an eyebrow at Cleo.

"It's okay," Cleo conceded. "Thanks for trying."

"Barkley eats *everything*," Jay said to the crowd. "Just like me." More laughs. He tugged on his pants, trying to get them up.

Cleo turned to her friends, ready to get the spotlight back where it belonged. "If you thought *that* was exciting, wait until you see what we've actually planned!"

She opened the door and her guests filed in: Caylee and Tessa first; then Anusha, with her mom's thick eyebrows; Lily, with her dad's long face and big-boned stature; Steffy, with her mom's wide smile and almond-shaped eyes; Rosa, with her dad's light brown complexion; Jasmine, with her mom's blocky figure and long black hair; Amelie, with her mom's auburn hair and willowy body; and Mia, with her mom's identical tinkling laugh.

Cleo couldn't help wondering: *How did she and her birth dad look alike? Would they look alike? Or sound alike? Maybe even* act *alike?*

She could think about that later. Everyone had made it into the family room. It was time for power makeovers! Just like on *Fortune.*

Cleo flung her arms wide. "Welcome to Salon Perfecto! Where everything we do is as close to perfection as possible." Some of the girls giggled. It felt good to be in charge again. "Your sleepover stylists this evening will be Mia and"—she gave a flamboyant flick of her hands and then rested them on her chest, feeling very Fortune-like— "*moi.* Who would like to be our first two clients?" All the girls raised their hands. Cleo didn't want anyone to feel hurt. "We'll go alphabetical. Amelie and Anusha—you first. And feel free to give suggestions. We're open to ideas, right, Mia?"

Mia nodded. "Sure." She plugged in her flat iron and Cleo's mom's curling iron.

Caylee spoke. "Did you want to do the 'before' and 'after' pictures?"

"How could I forget? Thank you, Caylee, Chief Operating Officer of Cleopatra Enterprises, Inc. What would I do without you?"

Caylee fluttered her eyelashes. "You're welcome. And I don't know."

Cleo found Dad telling Mom about his soccer team's game in the living room. "Dad! We need you and your camera in our makeover salon. Right away."

Dad hopped up and saluted. "Yes, boss." He pulled her into a hug. "But not until I get one of these!"

Cleo let him hug her, then hurried back to the family room. Amelie and Anusha were settled in the "salon chairs." Caylee and Mia clipped towels around their shoulders like smocks.

Dad came in with his camera and took all of their "before" shots. As soon as he was done, Cleo focused in on her work. She curled Anusha's hair a section at a time, her vision taking shape. She felt like a stylist on *Fortune*, helping Anusha to "make an impression" and tell the world who she was!

"Ooo! That turned out so cute!" Tessa said of Anusha's hair when Cleo had finished.

"Simple, yet elegant," Cleo said and handed Anusha the mirror.

Anusha smiled shyly at her reflection. Cleo had curled her shoulder-length hair into ringlets and then swept up the sides and secured them with rhinestone-studded star clips. "For just seven dollars the clips can be yours. We'll put your name on them, of course. I seem to recall your name means 'beautiful morning star.'" Cleo was working her magic.

Anusha nodded and her smile widened. "Okay," she said.

"Oh! I almost forgot." Cleo found the jar of glitter powder. "A little sparkle for the beautiful morning star?" she asked.

Anusha nodded again.

Cleo dusted the powder on Anusha's brown skin, giving it a sparkling sheen. She held the brush over Anusha's head and tapped it all around on her hair, as well. "Perfecto!" Cleo declared. Anusha giggled. She looked in the mirror once more and then it was Caylee's turn.

While working on Caylee, Cleo sensed the conversation dragging. The silences were becoming longer and more obvious. She grabbed the remote and turned on the TV. "Who else watches *Fortune?*"

None of the girls did, except Caylee, of course, who only watched it with Cleo. Some of the girls' moms did.

"You're going to love it!" She found the menu and went to the first recorded episode she had saved from the past week. "Caylee and I have been so busy working on Passion Clips, I haven't had time to watch the show every day like I usually do."

Most of the girls watched, although now and then some of them would talk when it wasn't a commercial, which annoyed Cleo, but she let it go. She was having a Passion Clips party with nine girls and everyone was having fun!

At the end, Mia and Cleo did each other's hair. When they were done, and all the "after" pictures had been taken, and Mom and Dad had *oohed* and *aahed* over how pretty they all were, and Josh and Jay had made a scene about how girly they all looked, it was time for pizza. And they were famished!

Thankfully, Mom took Josh and Jay upstairs for an Iron Man movie, and Barkley was locked in with them, or dog slobber would have been all over the pizza.

While the girls ate, they talked about how Max Peacock had gotten in trouble in PE for running around with his pogo stick as if it were a lance, challenging people to joust; and about how gross Rowdy Jimmy Ryerson was. At lunch that day, he had snorted a spaghetti noodle up his nose.

Tessa had been sitting next to him. "He had one end hanging out his nose, and the other end coming out of his mouth. He pulled it back and forth like floss!" The girls all shrieked in disgust. Cleo did too, although honestly, when she'd seen him doing it, she'd been impressed.

After that, it was quiet except for the pizza being gobbled. Chewing became the loudest sound in the room. Everyone looked at everyone else. The room exploded with laughter.

When it got quiet again, Amelie spoke: "What's it like being adopted?" She was looking at the picture of Cleo's family on the wall. The room was silent again, except for the sound of pizza crusts moving around in people's mouths. Cleo's ears felt plugged with cotton. Her brain felt fuzzy and her chest got tight. Normally, she felt great about being at the center of a group's attention, but not like this.

No one else here was adopted. Everyone waited to hear her response.

She shrugged. "It's no big deal. And it's all I've ever known, so . . ."

"So you were adopted as a baby?" Lily asked.

"Uh-huh." Cleo kept her eyes on the piece of pepperoni in front of her mouth.

"Do you know why your parents didn't keep you?" Mia asked. Cleo shook her head.

"Were they young?" Steffy asked.

"Kind of."

Amelie's question had opened a floodgate. Suddenly, they all had something they wanted to know about her adoption.

"My cousin's adopted," Tessa said. "My parents told us it's just another way some people get a family. It's not better or worse—just different."

Cleo was feeling different all right. And it seemed as if her brain had stopped sending messages to her mouth. For once in her life, she had *no idea* what to say.

"Jeremy's lucky, I think," Tessa continued. "He's got four parents who care about him."

"What do you mean?" Jasmine asked. "*Four* parents?"

"Oh, because he knows his birth parents. He does things with his birth dad sometimes, and his birth mom comes to a lot of our family things."

"Isn't that awkward?" Mia asked.

This *conversation* was awkward, and Cleo wanted it to end. Now.

Mia turned to Cleo. "Do your birth parents come to your family events?"

"Maybe she doesn't really want to talk about this," Caylee said quietly.

Thank you, Caylee.

"Do you?" Mia asked.

Cleo would be calm, cool, and collected—professional. Like Fortune. "Like I said, it's no big deal. Who wants ice cream?" She jumped up.

Everyone cheered at the suggestion of dessert.

"I'll get the sundae bar set up. Put your trash in here." She held up the bag Mom had left them and hurried out of the room.

The rest of the night she tried hard to forget about the conversation. *It's no big deal,* she repeated to herself. She folded paper fortune-tellers along with everyone else, but how could a little piece of paper tell her what she really wanted—needed—to know? What would it be like to meet her birth dad? Did she really want to do that? And where was her birth mom? Would she ever meet *her*?

After the lights were finally out and the whispers had been replaced by slow, heavy exhales around the room, Cleo snuck up to her bed and grabbed Beary. She went to her brothers' slightly ajar door and called quietly, "Come here, Barkley." His collar jangled as he shook out his body. He appeared at the door.

"Hi, boy!" she said, hugging him around his neck. He licked her face. She led him downstairs and between still bodies in sleeping bags. She scooted into her bag and squeezed Beary to her chest. Barkley plopped down alongside her. He sniffed her face and sneezed twice, probably from the glitter powder.

Dad had told Cleo once that dogs could smell if another dog had come from the same gene pool—if they were related by blood.

That would be a totally different kind of superpower. Cleo wished she had it.

She said a short prayer that she would know what to do about meeting her birth dad. If she did meet him, a relative-sniffing superpower wouldn't be necessary. He'd be able to tell her all about her birth family. So was she ready for that?

CHAPTER 14

Pest Zoo

Cleo awoke to high-pitched shrieks.

Amelie ran in place on the love seat. "A mouse just ran across my sleeping bag!" She gripped her crossed arms. "Ew! Ew! Ew!"

Everyone started screaming. A few girls burrowed into their bags; several others jumped onto the couch. Caylee sprang into the recliner without touching the floor.

Cleo stood quickly. Her sleeping bag slid to the ground. Barkley was gone. "Where?" she shouted. The mouse had been at large for weeks. Why did it have to choose *now* of all times to make its grand appearance?

"It went under there!" Amelie pointed in the direction of the couch. Lily, Jasmine, Steffy, and Mia, standing on the couch, squealed and hugged one another in fright.

Rosa sat up in her spot. She rubbed her eyes. Apparently, she was just getting the memo that a rodent was on the loose in their sleeping quarters. "It's just a mouse. What's the big deal?"

Cleo looked at Rosa. Now here was a girl with some sense. How had she and Cleo never become friends? After this experience, Cleo would have to change that.

"Hel-*lo*!" Mia scoffed. "*Just* a mouse? Who knows what it was doing in the middle of the night while we were innocently sleeping. It could have chewed off pieces of our hair for its nest or pooped in our sleeping bags!"

Anusha gasped. Tessa screamed. They shot from their bags and joined those already on the couch.

"I agree with Rosa," Cleo said. "Caylee sleeps with a bigger rodent every night."

"Tye-Dye's in a cage." Caylee sat tightly curled in the recliner. "That's totally different!"

Something small, gray, and furry scampered along the wall and disappeared behind the media center.

Cheese sticks and Chili's!

Everyone, except Rosa, screamed again. Even Cleo. She couldn't help it. It was just so . . . *mousy.*

"What's going on?" Mom appeared at the doorway in her robe, bed head and all. It dawned on Cleo that it was early. *Really* early. The sky was still darkish. Next door, Miss Jean's rooster crowed.

"It's the mouse," Cleo said forcefully, hoping Mom heard the frustration in her voice.

"*The* mouse?" Mia looked aghast. "It, like, lives here? You knew about it and you didn't kill it?"

"Everyone, pack up your stuff." Mom took charge. "Party's moving."

Cleo grabbed her sleeping bag, making sure Beary was stuffed out of view. She helped Anusha, who seemed the most afraid to leave the couch, carry her things. She whispered to Mom as she passed, "You *have* to get more traps in here—*today.* This is a social catastrophe of ginormous proportions from which I may never recover!"

"Exaggeration won't help the situation, Cleo."

Cleo ignored her and passed through the kitchen to

the living room. No one sat on the floor. They perched on the couch, the rocking chair, the dining chairs, or the fireplace's built-in brick bench, their feet curled up underneath them.

"Hey! Who's ready to star in a commercial?" she said with forced enthusiasm. No one raised a hand. They just glanced nervously at one another.

"Come on. We're not going to let a little mouse stop us!"

Caylee put her feet down first. "I'm ready."

Yes! Her faithful friend and business partner, coming through again.

"Caylee, you stay here with Amelie, Jasmine, Steffy, and Mia. Mia, you can use the bathroom through there to touch up everyone's hair." She pointed to the archway that led to the bathroom and spare bedroom-office.

"I'm not going back into the *mouse pit* to get the irons." Mia looked disgusted.

"I'll get them," Cleo said. "Anusha, Lily, Rosa, and Tessa, bring your clothes and come with me. We'll get ready in my bedroom." She had cleared the floor Friday morning, so it was decent.

Cleo ran and got the irons. No sign of Mickey, thank goodness.

She gave the flat iron to Mia, and took the curling one for herself, saying they'd switch when they were done using them. She told her group to follow her and headed for the stairs.

"A little morning excitement, huh?" Dad said as they passed through the kitchen. He was getting the coffee-maker going and had out all the stuff to make chocolate chip pancakes. Good. Chocolate chip pancakes should win her back a few social points.

"Not exactly the kind I was hoping for," Cleo said, feeling irked. She stomped up the stairs. At the doorway to her room, she stopped. Tipped on its side, on the floor near her desk, lay the mealworm container with the lid off. Oat bran was everywhere.

"Is that what I think it is?" Tessa asked.

Cleo hurtled across her room. She picked up the empty container. "Those little termites!" she hollered.

"Mealworms aren't termites," Lily said. "Are they?"

Cleo pushed past her friends and went to her brothers' closed door. *Pound-pound-pound.* "Josh! Jay! What did you do with my mealworms?"

No answer.

"Mom! *Mom!* Josh and Jay stole my science assignment!"

The door opened a crack. "No we didn't." It was Josh.

Cleo pushed all the way in. Barkley got to his feet, his tail wagging and his muzzle covered in evidence. Oat bran. "Barkley! What did you do?" She sensed the other girls standing in the door behind her.

"It's not his fault." Jay stood next to Barkley, his arm draped over their black lab. He dropped his chin and mumbled, "Sorry, Cleo."

"What did *you* do?"

"I just wanted to hold one."

"Of my mealworms? You shouldn't have done that without asking."

"I know."

"So where are they? Did Barkley *eat* them?"

Josh looked serious. "We think so."

Cleo crossed her arms angrily. She would have to tell Mr. B her dog ate her homework after all.

"Except for one," Josh said.

"One?" Cleo asked. "Well, where is it?"

Jay mumbled something.

"What did you say?" Cleo couldn't have heard him right.

"I ate it," Jay said quietly.

"Ew!!!" More screams from her party guests.

"You *what?*" Cleo shrieked. Could this day get any worse? And it wasn't even 8:00 a.m.! "Why did you do that?"

Her friends were freaking out about how gross her brother was.

Jay burst into tears and bolted from the room.

"Get back here!" Cleo yelled. "You little bug!" No way were her brothers getting DinoFormers from her after this craziness. She turned to go after him. The girls parted like the Red Sea. She was ruined!

She met Mom and Dad on the stairs. Mom had Jay in her arms. "*Now* what's going on?"

"Jay and Barkley ate my mealworms!"

"What? When?" Mom tried to get Jay to look at her, but his face was buried in her neck.

"Excuse us, girls," Dad said. "Why don't you wait downstairs? We have some family business to tend to."

Cleo's friends glanced at her as they passed, seeming relieved to be released from the scene of the grisly crime. Cleo followed her parents to the boys' room. She crossed her arms and smoldered at her family. First, the mouse. Then her mealworms. At the one time when she *most* wanted to make a good impression. She really *did* live in a pest zoo!

Dad began asking questions. Jay wouldn't talk, so Josh became his spokesperson, telling them what Jay had told him: The night before, Jay had been curious to know what a mealworm tasted like (since Dad had said people ate them), so he ate one. He must not have closed the lid all the way, because that morning they had found Barkley with his nose in the container. The mealworms were gone.

"But we don't know for sure that he ate them," Dad said.

"Knowing Barkley, I think we can be pretty sure," Mom said, eyeing the dog.

Barkley whimpered. He was either sorry or about to throw up.

"Can I go?" Cleo asked. "My guests are waiting."

"Jay, you owe your sister an apology for getting into her things," Dad said.

For once, Cleo wasn't the one in the hot seat for taking something that wasn't hers.

Jay finally spoke. "I'm sorry, Cleo."

"Okay." She was still mad, but she had to know one thing. "What'd it taste like, anyway?"

Jay's face scrunched. "Squishy."

Cleo shivered at the thought of a wiggly *Tenebrio molitor* in her mouth. Disgusting.

So much for Steve Jobs and the businessworms. But maybe Jay had done her a favor. With her subjects gone, she wouldn't have to spend any more time on *that* assignment!

CHAPTER 15

Ad Shoot — Take One

Chocolate chip pancakes with canned whipped cream worked exactly as Cleo had hoped. Like a charm. Everything was looking up again.

She and her nine new best friends—bonded by the events of the last fifteen hours—walked to Wilson Park, laughing about how scared Amelie had looked when she'd first spotted the mouse and about Jay eating a mealworm. A *mealworm*! Crazy kid.

Mom and Dad were letting them go without a parent, one, because they were such a large group, and two, because Ernie Junior, Caylee's thirteen-year-old brother, was coming along as cameraman. He wanted to be a filmmaker, so he was excited to help them with the project.

Cleo, excited to be a film *director*, started giving orders as soon as they got to the playground. "Tessa and Steffy, I want you on the two-person, bouncy seesaw thing. Anusha, Lily, and Jasmine on the swings. The rest of you pick a spot on the jungle gym."

"Can I be on the monkey bars, instead?" Steffy the gymnast asked. "I can climb on top, hang upside down . . ."

"Okay. Mia, you go with Tessa on the bouncy seesaw."

"That thing is for little kids. I want to be on the swings."

Cleo huffed. Her "irk levels" were rising again.

"I'll be with Tessa," Caylee offered.

"Okay, okay. Fine. Tessa and Caylee on the bouncy see-saw. Mia to the swings with Anusha and Jasmine. Steffy—monkey bars. Lily, Rosa, and Amelie—jungle gym. Are we cool?" Thankfully, everyone nodded.

Cleo was just about to yell, "Passion Clips ad—take one!" when two boys about Jay's age ran onto the playground. They chased each other around. A couple of women who looked like their moms lagged behind. They talked and sipped coffees, not paying attention to the boys.

"Excuse me!" Cleo shouted at the boys. "We're using this site for an ad shoot. We need you to stay off the playground—just until we're done."

The boys kept running around, as if they hadn't even heard her. "Just a minute," she said to the others. She made a beeline to the two moms. "Excuse me," she said as politely as she could, "my friends and I are shooting a commercial for my business, and I'm wondering if you could have your kids play on the grass or somewhere else until we're done? It won't be too long."

One of the women cocked her head. Her eyes were narrowed and one eyebrow was raised. She definitely wasn't sold.

Before Cleo had a chance to woo her with Persuasion Power, the other woman jumped in. "Shooting a commercial! How cool!" She looked at her friend. "Can you believe kids today? So enterprising. And talk about technologically *savvy*. Way ahead of where we were as kids. Don't you love it?"

The tough-customer woman still looked skeptical, but

she murmured agreement. That was all Cleo needed. "Thank you so much! We really appreciate it. You're totally welcome to watch. Do you have daughters, or nieces, perhaps? Because if you do, you might be interested in our product, *Passion Clips*, to tell the world who you are!"

The women weren't really listening. They were calling and motioning to their sons to come with them. The mom who had been agreeable from the start pulled a football out of a big bag and held it up like bait. The boys zoomed toward her, one of them grabbing the ball as he passed, and they were off to the field to play catch.

"Thank you!" Cleo called after them.

"Good luck with your commercial," the friendly mom said, walking away.

Cleo scanned the playground. Her friends were mostly just sitting around. Steffy was hanging upside down on the bars. Mia, Jasmine, and Anusha were swinging.

"Okay, everyone, we're ready." No one moved. "Places, people!" Girls lumbered to their feet, looking suddenly tired. They *had* been awoken early that morning. She felt irritated again that her parents hadn't taken care of their little rodent problem sooner.

But that was then. This was now. And right *now*, she needed to make a commercial that would knock Fortune's socks off!

She wished she had one of those clapper things to get the camera rolling (and the talent moving). She envisioned herself wearing a pair of clapper barrettes. *Yes!* Caylee could make her a pair of clapper Passion Clips. Moviemaking was officially one of her new passions.

"What about you?" Caylee asked. "Where are you going to be?"

Cleo chortled. "Oh yeah. I almost forgot myself!" Of course she needed to be in the ad. She wanted Fortune to see her too! She climbed onto the jungle gym and positioned herself at the top of the slide.

"What are we supposed to do?" Lily wanted to know.

"Just look like you're having fun," Cleo answered. "And try to keep your Passion Clips aimed at the camera at all times."

"Isn't it the cameraman's job to make sure he gets shots of our hair?" Rosa pointed out.

Cleo bristled. Why was this girl telling her how to direct *her* ad? She puffed her chest. "Actually, it's the director's job." She turned to Ernie Junior (who could be called that only in her head—he'd punch her if she said it out loud). "Lots of close-ups of the clips, cameraman. Got it?"

"Got it." He had his handheld video camera ready to go.

"We could dance," Rosa suggested, breaking into the Nae Nae on the wobbly bridge.

Amelie almost fell over. "Hey! Careful!"

This wasn't supposed to be commercial-making by committee, but Cleo had to admit dancing was a good idea. "Okay. But only dance if you aren't going to look like a dork."

"That's not a very nice thing to say," Lily said.

The pancakes and whipped cream seemed to be wearing off. Time to get this show on the road!

She was shouting, "Passion Clips commercial for FortuneTube, take one!" when E.J.'s cell phone rang. Cleo expected him to silence it—he was on the job, after all—but he answered.

Cleo clapped her hands to her head and let out a low growl.

Flapjacks and Facebook! Time was ticking! They didn't have all day. Parents would be arriving at Cleo's house in just over an hour.

While E.J. talked, the talent got antsy. Rosa took on

the role of the mouse in Cleo's house and started chasing everyone around the playground. Girls were screeching and jumping off and onto the jungle gym. Any minute, more random people could show up and Cleo would be back at square one, trying to convince more adults to keep their kids away while they filmed.

Cleo widened her eyes in exasperation, but E.J. just turned his back, plugged his ear, and walked farther away. She wished she had one of those director's chairs. The picnic table would have to do, but she couldn't sit—she was too short. She stood on top, summoning all of her directorial powers.

"Back to your places, everyone! Let's run a rehearsal." Hadn't Lexie said they had to rehearse before shooting the Sunshine Sparkle commercial? A lot, if Cleo remembered right. They were going to do this like the professionals.

"We *are* rehearsing," Jasmine said. "You said to look like we're having fun and that's what we're doing!"

"What is there to rehearse?" Lily said. "We're just going to dance around." She did a silly dance move, making everyone, except Cleo—and Ernie Junior, who was still on the stupid phone—laugh.

"*I'm* the director!" she yelled.

"*Dictator* is more like it," Mia snapped. "You don't need to be so pushy."

"I'm not being pushy! I'm trying to film a commercial!"

"Well, it's not very fun." Mia jumped down from the jungle gym steps.

"I agree," Amelie said.

The others looked around uncomfortably. No one came to her defense. Not even Caylee. Ernie Junior's voice rose and fell as he laughed and talked with whoever it was that was more important than Cleo's ad shoot.

"We have a lot of clip orders to fill before tomorrow, Cleo," Caylee said. She shrugged apologetically. "Maybe we should be making those instead?"

Cleo felt her insides starting to unravel, but she steeled herself and kept pressing forward. "But this is going to be on FortuneTube!" She didn't like the sound of desperation that had crept into her voice. "It's super important!"

"To *you*," Steffy said. "We're your friends, remember? Not your employees."

"Yeah, last time I checked, no one was paying me two thousand dollars to be here," Mia complained.

Cleo's temper flared at the comparison to Lexie Lewis. "But you were all excited about it. You wanted to do it."

"We *did*," Amelie said, "until you started bossing us around."

Tessa looked at her watch. "Sorry, Cleo, but I have to get back soon. My dad is picking me up for my horse-riding lesson in fifteen minutes."

"Already?" Cleo hadn't realized Tessa needed to leave earlier than the others.

"Me too," Steffy said. "Gymnastics."

Cleo was losing two of her three most outgoing, charismatic, willing-to-dance-around-and-be-silly girls. The other one, Mia, still looked sour. Cleo didn't particularly feel like hamming it up for the camera herself. "Fine. We won't do it."

E.J. got off the phone as the girls drifted from the playground. "Hey, where's everyone going? We haven't shot anything."

"The shoot's over," Cleo said. *And the party,* she thought. *And probably all of my friendships too.*

CHAPTER 16
Friends Forever!™

C leo was distraught. Everyone had left her house amid uncomfortable silence and short good-byes. Mom tried to get Cleo to talk about what had happened at the park, but Cleo didn't want to, and fortunately (with Dad's encouragement), Mom didn't push it.

She lay on her bed, wondering what had gone wrong. Persuasion was her superpower! Why hadn't it worked for her that morning? She looked up at Fortune, her thoughts leading her this way and that.

Okay, so she'd gotten a little intense. She got intense

186

sometimes. Maybe she'd even let the power of directing go to her head. The ugly truth reared up like a sea serpent from the depths of a murky lake. She'd been seeing her friends only as useful in helping her to achieve her ends. Again.

Ugh. She would have to say she was sorry. She hated saying she was sorry. But it was the only way to make things better. She hoped people would forgive her, and not so they would buy more clips or be in her commercial (which she was determined to try shooting again), but because she wanted to be their friend.

She quickly wrote an apology to Caylee (notes were better for apologies than face-to-face, at least initially), loaded it into her Canine Carrier Capsule™ and called for Barkley. She attached the capsule to the Velcro that Mom had helped her sew onto his collar and sent him off. "Take this to Caylee. Go!" She pointed up the street and Barkley trotted down the porch steps and out the front gate, not as speedily as she wished, but the message would get there, eventually.

Twenty or so minutes later, Barkley came back with a reply. I forgive you ♥ ♥ ♥. Want to come over and play with Tye-Dye?

So Cleo asked her parents and went over to Caylee's. They still had most of her church family's orders to fill and a few from Saint Bart's. But first, she held Tye-Dye, who was softer than Josh's blankie, Mom's hair, and Cleo's lucky rabbit's foot combined. Cleo could have held him all afternoon, but she remembered he could only handle a few minutes at a time and put him back for his sake. She didn't want him to get stressed.

By the time she left, Cleo felt a whole lot better. First, she had told Caylee about the prospect of meeting her birth father, and Caylee, as usual, had listened really well and said all the right things, like, "No matter what happens, you know I'll still be your BFF." It felt good to have someone besides her parents sharing the load of her big news, at last.

Second, not only had they completed eight sets of clips, they had come up with a new product line: Friends Forever!™—clips personalized with the names of two forever friends. They'd even created a prototype: interlocking hearts, featuring their names, of course. Not bad for a day's work.

Monday came and Cleo had more apologizing and explaining to do. First, she had to tell Mr. Boring about the tragic end that had come to her mealworms. Even though all the girls already knew, she waited until recess to bring it up with her teacher because she didn't want the class to make a big deal of it. She'd experienced enough embarrassment over the whole thing.

He understood but she would still need to do a report based on whatever data she'd collected before the worms' untimely end. Then he sent her outdoors to get the "ants out of her pants."

"And the mealworm squiggles out of my middle!" Cleo called as she left the room.

When she got outside, she realized she didn't want to have to repeat her apology multiple times and she definitely didn't want to write it out eight times. The only thing to do was to ask everyone to meet on the hillside after lunch. She would talk to them all at once. Caylee offered to help spread the word, which meant they each had only four girls to find.

Cleo found three of her four girls easily. Anusha, Rosa, and Lily were hanging out together. Everything seemed about the same as it had before the sleepover, which meant they didn't have much to say. But they agreed to meet her on the hill.

Next she had to find Mia, the one who had spearheaded the walkout. Cleo spotted her doing flips on the high bar. Lexie Lewis sat on the bar right below. Great.

Caylee appeared at Cleo's side. "Done," she said. "They all said they'd be there." Her eyes went to where Cleo was looking. "You could find Mia at lunch," she suggested.

"She'll probably be sitting with Lexie there too," Cleo said. "They always sit together."

Caylee let out a long breath. "Yeah. Want me to come with you?"

Cleo nodded and charged ahead. "Hey, Mia," she said, walking up on the opposite side from where Lexie sat.

"Hey." Mia's eyes didn't meet hers.

"I was wondering if you'd come over to the hill after lunch. Me and the others . . ." She shut her mouth. It wouldn't be considerate to mention the sleepover in front of Lexie, if she really did feel left out.

"The others?" Mia asked.

"Yeah, you know . . . from Friday night." She avoided looking at Lexie.

"Not if you're planning on trying to get us to shoot your ad again."

Lexie, still perched atop the bar, barely stifled a laugh.

"Well, I was going to see . . ." Mia didn't look in the "buying" mood. Cleo changed course quickly. "But that's not really why I want to meet. It's for . . . um, something else." She definitely wasn't going to mention her planned apology in front of Lexie.

"Can't you just tell me now?" Mia flipped around the bar once and landed on her feet.

Feeling on the spot, Cleo did the thing that came most naturally to her. "Actually, I think this is something you might both be interested in," she said, looking at Lexie for the first time. "Caylee and I are introducing a new line of Passion Clips: Friends Forever!—trademark."

"You can't trademark that." Lexie crossed her arms. She wobbled and grabbed the bar again. "Everyone says it all the time."

"Doesn't matter. If it's not been claimed, I can claim it. And I looked it up last night, and it hasn't been claimed. So the name is all mine. I mean, *ours*." She and Caylee exchanged smiles.

"You act like you're an actual company president, but

you're not," Lexie said, jumping down from the bar. "You're just another fifth-grader selling homemade stuff. And that tooth-pulling business . . . what'd you make before you barfed all over everyone and *attacked* me? Fifty cents?"

Ooo . . . this girl. It took everything Cleo had not to slug her again.

"Fifth-graders *can* run companies." Caylee's eyes were fierce, her fists clenched, her head cocked with a definite attitude. "We saw a girl on *Fortune* whose natural-hair-care products are sold in thirty-five stores across five states, so there!"

"Was she ten?" Lexie challenged.

"No, she was fifteen. But that's technically still a kid. And anyway, you act like *you're* a TV star and you're just another fifth-grader who's done a commercial. So why don't you just leave Cleo alone already?"

Go, Caylee! Cleo was seriously surprised . . . and impressed. *And* she had just gotten a fantabulous idea!

"Look, Lexie, couldn't we just call a truce?" It was how Dad got the boys to make up: *calling a truce.* It was another way of saying, "Wipe the slate clean, start fresh." Or as they said at church, "Every day is a new beginning."

Lexie hadn't laughed in her face, or turned and walked. Cleo forged ahead. "We both have our dreams. Maybe we could help each other achieve our goals."

For a second, it looked like Lexie was choking on a mealworm. "And how would we do that exactly?"

"Well . . . I want to make a commercial. You want to be in commercials. Maybe you could . . . be in my commercial?" She said the last part fast before she chickened out.

There was an uncomfortable silence. Cleo rushed to fill it. "I'm submitting it to FortuneTube."

Cleo couldn't read Lexie's expression. Would she mock her again? Grab Mia and walk away?

"Why would I do that?" Lexie asked.

The pitch of Cleo's voice rose with her eyebrows. "It could be seen by"—she stretched out her words—"*thousands* of people." More silence.

"Maybe." The word popped from Lexie's mouth like a clown from a jack-in-the-box.

"No, definitely! It *could* be seen by thousands of people," Cleo urged.

"I mean, maybe I'll do it." Lexie folded her arms.

"What? Oh! Okay." Honestly, Cleo had been expecting an automatic "No way!"

"When are you going to do it?" Lexie asked.

Cleo turned to Caylee. She didn't want to leave her partner out of a business decision, but Caylee just shrugged.

"How about this Saturday? Wilson Park," Cleo suggested.

"I have to check with my mom to see if I have any auditions that day. But if I'm free"—she let out a big sigh—"I guess I'll do it."

"Great!" Maybe she shouldn't have sounded so excited to work with a girl who'd been mean to her in the past, but Cleo couldn't help it—she was an enthusiastic person.

As they walked back to class, Cleo linked her arm with Caylee's. "Thanks for standing up for me, Jelly. That was amazing."

"I thought I was going to faint."

"You didn't *look* like you were going to. You were awesome! And I hope you didn't mind me announcing our new product line before running it by you first. I just sort of flip into selling mode sometimes, like Diana Prince becoming Wonder Woman." Dad loved all those corny old cartoons.

Caylee laughed. "Of course I didn't mind. It's your superpower!"

After lunch, Cleo stood before her sleepover guests sitting on the grassy hill and apologized. She asked them to consider joining her for take two of the ad shoot—completely voluntary, of course. Then she told them about Friends Forever Passion Clips, took three orders on the spot, and declared that she would be "friends forever" with all of them!

CHAPTER 17

A Social Media Star Is Born

That week, Mom helped Cleo and Caylee get set up on the crafters' website Artsy, since they didn't have time, money, or the expertise to create their own website just yet.

Friday, Cleo turned in her book report on *The Great Gilly Hopkins*. She'd tried to stop reading it, but she couldn't. She needed to know whether Gilly's birth mom had come back. When she'd gotten to the end, Cleo had been so mad she'd thrown the book to the ground. She'd wanted to rip out the last few pages, but the book was the school library's, and Ms. Tomasello would make her pay for damages.

Reading *Gilly* had made her wonder even more if she should say yes to meeting her birth dad. What if it went horribly? What if he appeared only to disappear again and never return? She still hadn't told her parents what she wanted to do, but they weren't rushing her, and besides, she had her ad to finish. Even more important, she had Fortune's attention to get!

Saturday came, and Cleo was ready. They met at the park, everyone except Lily and Rosa, who had conflicts. Miraculously, the playground was empty. The skies were sunny and blue, and the air was perfectly warm. Surely these were all signs that today's shoot would be a success. If any strangers showed up to play, Cleo was prepared to ask them (politely, of course) to stay off the equipment until they were done—and if there were parents with girls, she would sell them Passion Clips. The proof of their product's quality (not to mention their popularity) was everywhere that morning!

The girls fixed each other's hair and made sure their clips were easy to be seen. Tessa wore her horses; Mia her chef hat and spoon; Anusha her sparkling star. Jasmine had in her soccer balls, Steffy sported her pink balance beams, and Amelie wore her microphones.

Caylee had chosen her Tye-Dye the Hamster clip, and she'd brought two new Passion Clips for Cleo: a fun spider with black pipe-cleaner legs and a glittery, silver spider-web. *Persist* was written in black puff paint across the face of the web.

"Itsy-Bitsy!" Cleo exclaimed.

"You're passionate about spiders?" Tessa asked.

"It's not just any spider. It's *Itsy-Bitsy.* Because I never give up, of course!"

"Ohhh!" they all said at once. Everyone agreed it was perfect for Cleo.

Cleo and her mom had put Cleo's hair into two pom-pom puffs that morning. Caylee carefully removed Cleo's lightbulb barrette and replaced it with Itsy-Bitsy on one side of her part and the spiderweb on the other.

"Thanks, Jelly." Cleo put her arm around Caylee, grateful for her forever friend.

"Are we ready?" E.J. asked. He palmed his handheld videocam.

"Did you turn off your phone?" Cleo asked. Thankfully, the phone was nowhere in sight, but she didn't want it ringing in the middle of the shoot. Knowing Ernie Junior, he'd pick up the call and they'd have to start all over.

He pulled the phone from his pocket and powered it off.

"Thanks," Cleo said. "I guess we're ready. Except Lexie's not here. She told me yesterday she was coming. Did she say anything to you, Mia?"

Mia shook her head. "No."

She probably changed her mind, Cleo thought. *Oh well, I tried.* She was about to call, "Places, everyone!"— this time, she'd tell people to go wherever they wanted on the playground—when a silver Jaguar pulled up to the curb.

The car sparkled so brightly in the sun it hurt to look at, but they stared anyway. Lexie Lewis was in the backseat, looking like a movie star being chauffeured. Cleo took a deep breath and reminded herself she had invited the girl to join them. The past was the past.

Lexie got out and Cleo spied a little girl sitting in a car seat behind the driver. That must be their cousin, Neecie. Lexie shut her door and the front passenger window slid down. "Sparkle and shine, baby! You're a star in the making!"

Lexie barely looked back. "Okay! Bye!"

As soon as she got to the edge of the playground, the other girls (except Mia, who'd probably seen Lexie's mom and car before) were all over her: "Was that your mom?" "She looked like a model!" "Your car is so fancy!"

The jealousy bug was biting, but Cleo had determined she wouldn't let it get the best of her. "Wow, Lexie. Your mom *is* beautiful!" she burst out. Cleo had caught only a glimpse, but the woman was movie-star gorgeous, for sure.

Lexie rolled her eyes. "So I'm always told." She wore a gauzy, angel-sleeved, fuchsia top over a white camisole and white capris pants. The blouse's neckline sparkled with opalescent sequins. Her Hollywood star Passion Clip sparkled in her pressed-straight hair.

"Is your mom an actress?" Amelie asked.

"I guess. Bit parts. She's more focused on managing *my* career than her own, at this point."

Was Lexie bragging again? Or had Cleo detected a hint of resentment in what Lexie had said?

"Okay, everyone!" Cleo refocused on the group. "Today, we're here to have fun. I *promise.* So turn on your charm and let your passion shine! We're going to get

Ms. Fortune A. Davies to *notice* us!" She turned to Caylee. "Music, please."

Caylee tapped on her iPad screen to bring up the playlist that she and Cleo had created to inspire them during the shoot. Music came from the mini-speaker Caylee had also brought.

"Passion Clips FortuneTube ad—take *two*," Cleo said, jumping into position on the jungle gym. "And . . . ACTION!"

The girls danced and swung and slid and bounced to the music. E.J. circled the jungle gym and wove in and out of the swings and around the seesaw, getting footage of them all. When they were done, everyone was breathing hard, but they were all giggling and smiling.

"That was awesome!" Steffy said.

"Totally fun," Tessa agreed.

Even Lexie Lewis gave the shoot two thumbs-up.

Eventually all the parents stopped by to pick up their kids. Except for Lexie's. They waited and waited, but still her mom didn't come.

"I need to get going," E.J. said, "if you want me to have this edited by tomorrow night."

"Definitely!" Cleo blurted.

"And I have to go with him," Caylee said. "Mom made me promise." E.J., Caylee, and Cleo had walked over from their street, which was only four blocks away.

Cleo had planned to use E.J.'s phone to get permission to go straight to Caylee's so she could be there to oversee E.J.'s editing job, but she knew she shouldn't leave Lexie at the park alone.

"Go ahead. I'll wait here with Lexie," Cleo said.

"I can take care of myself." Lexie's head waggled. The skin between her eyebrows was bunched together. She crossed her arms. "Anyway, I'm used to waiting." This time Cleo definitely had heard resentment.

"My mom would be mad if she found out I left you here on your own. And you wouldn't want to meet my mom when she's mad." She thought of how angry Mom had been when she'd heard what Lexie had said about Cleo's birth mom giving her away.

Lexie shrugged. "Whatever. It's your choice."

"Call me when you get home," Caylee said. "Maybe you can come over." She waved good-bye.

Cleo waved back, and then suddenly, it was only Lexie and her, sitting on a square picnic table, their feet resting on the attached bench. Cleo couldn't think of a single time when she had been alone with Lexie, this girl who had been a thorn in her side from the first day she'd arrived at New Heights Elementary in the middle of fourth grade.

She shifted on the table. She had no idea how to bridge the difference between her and Lexie, whose family's lifestyle was obviously so much more opulent than Cleo's family's, and whose parents were much, *much* more glamorous than Cleo's parents. The distance between them felt enormous. Uncrossable.

They'd never cleared the air after their run-in a couple of weeks before. Sure, they'd each said sorry in Principal Yu's office, but only because they'd had no other choice. Cleo wasn't planning to bring it up at this point. Everything had gone well at the shoot, and they were putting it all behind them. Turning over a new leaf. Enjoying a new beginning. Right?

Except, there *was* something she felt compelled to get cleared up.

"I heard Cole telling some boys your dad played professional baseball?"

"Yeah, so?"

"You said in Mr. Yu's office, you know, a couple of weeks ago . . ."

Lexie widened her eyes and gave her a look that said, *Spit it out already.*

"You said your dad was a lawyer . . . who could sue my family?"

"He *is* a lawyer. Do you think I would just make that up?" Her eyes narrowed into slits.

Uh-oh. And they had been making such progress. Did Cleo think she'd lied? "No! I don't know. I was just wondering."

"He's a sports lawyer." Lexie sighed. "And he probably wouldn't have sued you. But I was mad."

Cleo nodded. "So . . . did he play professional base-ball?"

"Yes! My brother's not a liar either. Our dad played in the minor leagues, on a farm team for the Phillies."

"Farm team? Like in a field with cows and chickens?"

Lexie threw back her head and laughed. "No! A farm team just means the place where players are groomed to play in the majors."

"Ohhh . . ." Cleo had a funny thought. "I was imagining a row of chickens laying baseballs." She giggled.

Lexie covered her mouth and snickered. "And cows catching fly balls!"

They looked at each other and laughed loudly.

Lexie sighed again, more lightheartedly this time. "Seriously, though, I think he spent one season playing in the majors. And it was before we were even born."

"I've never known anyone who played professional baseball, even for one season." Cleo grabbed Lexie's arm. "Hey, could I get your dad's autograph? My brother Josh is a *huge* baseball fan. He'd probably do nice things for me for a couple of *months* if I got him your dad's autograph."

Lexie looked doubtful, but then she smiled. "Sure, I guess. If you really want it."

Cleo nodded quickly. "Thanks."

The quiet stretched between them again. Cleo scanned the streets for the silver Jaguar. The sun made the exposed skin of her hair part feel too hot. "So, what movies has your mom been in? Any I would know?"

"Hardly," Lexie spluttered.

"I know lots of movies!" Cleo said defensively. Why was this girl bent on putting her down?

"I meant 'hardly,' as in she hasn't been in any movies. Just TV."

"Oh. Well, like what?"

"*Specter. Criminal Case. Neighborhood 9-1-1.*"

Cleo shrugged and shook her head. "Never heard of 'em. But that's no surprise. My parents don't let me watch nighttime dramas. I mainly just watch *Fortune.*"

Lexie chewed on her bottom lip. She looked as if she wanted to say something more, but instead she looked off into the distance.

"Do you want to be on TV shows too?" Cleo asked.

"*Of course.*" Her voice rose up and down, as if the answer was obvious. "I like doing auditions. I'm good at them. And shooting the juice commercial *was* fun. It's just . . ." She looked at her hands again.

"What?"

Lexie shrugged. "It's just lately I feel like the only time I have my mom's attention is when we're going to an audition. And then all we talk about is what I should do and shouldn't do. It's like all she cares about is me getting TV spots. Not *me.*"

Cleo nodded, even though this wasn't something she could relate to at all. From what she could tell, her mom was nothing like Lexie's. She for sure wasn't the Hollywood type.

"It's like I'm her project and Neecie is her daughter."

"But she's actually her niece, right?"

"Yeah, but she treats her more like a daughter than she does me. They're going to adopt her."

Cleo felt her eyes widen. "Really?"

"Really."

"Where are her parents?"

"My aunt Denise, my mom's sister, died pretty soon after my cousin was born. She had cancer while she was pregnant, but she didn't do chemo because she didn't want it to affect her baby. My uncle tried, but he couldn't take care of little Denise on his own, so my mom's parents had her for a couple of years. But then my grandma died too, and there was no way my grandpa could take care of a two-year-old. So my mom took her in."

"Wow. That's really sad . . . about your aunt, I mean."

"Yeah." Lexie nodded, keeping her eyes on her hands. "I know I shouldn't have said what I said . . ."

Cleo was confused. Did she mean she shouldn't have told Cleo her feelings about her mom? Or she shouldn't have talked about her family and Neecie?

"About your birth mom giving you away. I shouldn't have called you a freak."

Cleo sucked in her breath. "Oh!"

"I'm sorry." Lexie's words hung in the air, a half bridge that Cleo had to decide whether to complete.

The apology was genuine. Cleo could hear it in her voice. Suddenly, Lexie was a different girl, sitting there stooped with her hands clasped between her legs.

Cleo took a deep breath. Lexie Lewis had been so far out of line Cleo didn't think she could ever get back *in* line. "I'm sorry too . . . that I hit you." She couldn't believe she was apologizing.

"You got me good." Lexie rubbed her chin as if remembering the hit to her mouth.

Cleo wanted to say, "You deserved it," but instead she said, "I never hit anyone like that before."

"I guess no one ever made you that mad before."

"That's for sure." Cleo looked at her sideways. "But why are you apologizing now?"

Lexie looked up at a bird squawking in a nearby tree. The leaves rustled as the bird took off. "Like I said, I don't always like having my cousin around. Everything has changed since she came. I've been mad a lot since we changed schools—at my mom, at other kids, at Neecie. But then, I know she couldn't help what happened with her mom . . . and neither could you."

Cleo gripped the edge of the table. As soon as Lexie

had mentioned Neecie's mom, Cleo had felt as if she were leaving her body and floating away.

"I guess I'm just tired of being so mad . . . and mean. I'm tired of being enemies."

Cleo's whole self was there again, sitting next to Lexie, a real girl with problems and struggles, and not just a girl who wanted everyone to notice her or to be at the center of the universe. "Yeah, it's a lot more tiring than being friends." She held out her hand. "Apology accepted."

Lexie grasped Cleo's hand. "Me too."

They smiled at each other.

"So, you're going to have an adopted sister soon," Cleo said. "Hey! Maybe I could be a like a Big Buddy to Neecie, since I know what it's like to be adopted."

Lexie looked away.

"Of course," Cleo added hurriedly, "she probably won't need that because she's going to have such a splendarvelous big sister to look out for her."

Lexie's eyebrows arched. "Splendarvelous?"

"Yes." Cleo bobbed her head. "Splendid and marvelous."

Lexie gave her a crooked half smile. "An adopted Big Buddy . . . yeah. Maybe you could come over to my house some time and play with her."

"And with you, of course!"

Lexie smiled more fully at that.

"I know! We could watch *Fortune*! Fortune's a big dreamer, you know, just like us."

"Yeah . . . just like us." The silver Jaguar pulled up to the curb. "See you at school, Cleo." She hopped off the bench and walk-skipped toward her mom's car.

"See you at school!" Cleo called. Wow. She was pretty sure she had just experienced an actual miracle. Lexie Lewis had apologized. Cleo had apologized in return and meant it.

Yes. It was a miracle.

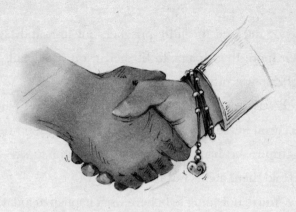

◆ CHAPTER 18 ◆
Meeting Mr. Banks

That night, after her brothers had gone to bed, Cleo sat with her parents in the family room, on the couch under their family portrait on the wall. The mouse had been caught earlier in the day—in a "smart trap" that Cleo wished she'd invented. The see-through, green little house had a way inside to the saltine-cracker bait lying there, but once the mouse was in, there was no way out, except when and where the house owner decided.

Cleo had missed all the action. Dad and the boys had

already released the little prisoner, but Josh and Jay had been more than happy to fill her in on the details. The Pest Zoo was officially closed.

It was quiet, except for the sound of Barkley's panting. He lay on her feet and looked up at her as if he sensed the big thing she had decided and was about to say—after she told them about Lexie.

"You're not going to believe what happened today," she looked back and forth between her parents.

Dad's eyes narrowed. "Let's see . . . you secured a venture capitalist for your latest business?"

"No, but I will. This, I *never* saw coming."

Mom's eyebrows popped. "Our daughter the visionary didn't see something coming? Tell me more."

"You won't believe it, Mom. It was a miracle. Maybe not as flashy as the Bible kind, but still, a miracle."

"Okay, you've got me. What happened?"

"Lexie Lewis apologized."

"That's great," Dad said.

"Do you think she really meant it?" Mom asked.

Cleo nodded vigorously. "Even more amazing, I apologized for hitting her. And *I* really meant it."

Mom put her arm around Cleo and squeezed. "Honey,

any time two people make up and mean it, that is definitely a miracle."

"There's more. Her family is adopting."

"Really?"

"That's what *I* said!" Cleo laughed. "They're adopting Lexie and Cole's cousin, Neecie. Denise. Named after their mom's sister." Her voice got quieter. "Who died."

Barkley whimpered as if he understood what Cleo had just said. Mom and Dad stayed quiet.

Cleo squirmed under Dad's gaze, which was so full of love she didn't know what to do with it all. And she didn't know if she could go through with what she had planned to say: that she wanted to meet her birth dad. That she sometimes felt like an alien child who'd come from outer space or like that teeny-tiny girl in the story Mom used to read to her, Thumbelina, who appeared magically out of a flower. Without people to whom she could attribute her presence in the world, without a story about where she came from *before* the foster mom's house, she felt cut off. Like a branch disconnected from its tree.

She plunged ahead. "Hearing about Neecie, and about her parents and what happened to her mom and thinking about how when she gets older she's going to *know* what happened," Cleo hesitated, "well, it made me think that I want to know too, for myself. I want to meet my birth dad." She looked into her dad's dark brown eyes. "If you're sure it's okay with you."

Dad pulled her into his arms. "It's absolutely, positively, one hundred percent okay with me. In fact, I was hoping that's what you'd want, because I want to meet him too!"

The next day, Cleo went over to Caylee's to view Ernie Junior's work on the ad. The edited video showed the girls having fun on the playground, interspersed with close-ups of the clips, all set to Caylee and Cleo's favorite upbeat song.

"It's good," Cleo said. "But it's missing something . . ." What would give it a little more *pop*? "I know! Pop-up bubbles! To show our thoughts! Could you do that?"

E.J. clicked a few times on the screen and a dialogue bubble appeared, which he positioned over Amelie's head.

"Yes!" Cleo said. "You're a genius, Ernie—I mean, E.J." She grimaced. "Sorry."

He knocked her with his elbow. "Watch it, Queen of the Nile."

Cleo grinned. She grabbed Caylee's arm and shook it in excitement. Caylee flopped around dramatically as if in an earthquake, and they both laughed hysterically.

They directed E.J. to fill in the bubbles with things like "I love to sing!" and "I'm the next Top Chef!" Lexie's bubble, highlighting her Hollywood star clip said, "Watch out, Hollywood, here I come!" which Cleo knew Lexie would love, in spite of how things were with her mom at the moment.

They ended the promo spot with their Artsy address and their logo: *Passion Clips*™ in the same curlicue font she'd used on their business cards with TELL THE WORLD WHO YOU ARE! in bold small caps underneath.

When they were done watching the final cut, Cleo threw her arms around E.J. "It's *fantastamazing*! Thank you!"

He scrunched his face and pulled away but didn't make too big a fuss. "All right, all right. I'm glad you like it."

"I don't like it. I *love-love-love* it!"

First thing the next morning, Fortune and her people

would find a Passion Clips ad uploaded to FortuneTube. Who knew what could happen next?

At the end of that week, Cleo came home from school with big news. Mr. Boring had let her show their FortuneTube ad in class, but even more exciting, the video had already been viewed more than a thousand times! Cleo dashed into the kitchen to tell Mom, who stood at the counter reading the label on a sealed bag of . . . Were those *mealworms*?

Cleo rushed over. "Don't tell me I have to redo my science project!" Then she saw that they weren't wriggling or squiggling. "They're dead."

"Yep. Although I think the manufacturer would prefer us to think of them as *dried*."

Cleo read the outside of the bag. "'Chubby Mealworms. One hundred percent natural dried mealworms.' *Ewwww*." She had a horrific thought. "You're not going to make us *eat* them, are you?"

Mom laughed. "No! Not yet, anyway. But after Barkley gobbled up your worms, I did a little research and Dad was right. Insects are the up-and-coming protein source. So, I thought, why not put them in Cleo's Canine Cookies, for added protein—and to make them stand out among all the fancy dog treats on the market these days."

Cleo looked at her skeptically. "You sure about that?"

"Not entirely. But I thought, why not? Let's take a risk! Maybe we'll be on the cutting edge of a huge trend."

Cleo nodded. "I like the way you're thinking, Mom."

Mom put her hand on Cleo's shoulder. "We heard back from Kelvin Banks."

A surge like an electric current shot through Cleo, warming her face and making her feel a little shaky.

"How would you like to meet him this Sunday after church?"

Cleo bit her lip. She felt short of breath. It was what she wanted, but she was scared too. "Will you and Dad be with me?"

"Of course!" Mom put her arms around Cleo. Cleo didn't move. She was growing up. She was even CEO of her own successful business. But she still needed her mom's hugs. She looked up into Mom's face.

"Could we buy me a new outfit first?"

Mom's brow furrowed. "Money's a bit tight after your party . . ."

Cleo nodded understandingly. "It's okay."

"But this is too important"—Mom's face relaxed—"not to find a way."

Cleo's smiling face matched her mom's.

Sunday, Cleo and her family barreled west on I-10, headed for Culver City. Cleo sat stiffly behind her brothers (who were singing "The Wheels on the Bus" at the tops of their lungs), clutching Beary and wearing her new clothes—a glittery gold tank top, a purple jean skirt, and gold-and-cream diamond-patterned leggings. The clothes had seemed so comfortable in the store. Now they felt itchy and tight.

The *best* purchase, and her new favorite article of clothing, had been the purple jean jacket with diamond rhinestone buttons and a rhinestone butterfly on the front. It had been a splurge, and Cleo had never loved her mom more than at the moment she'd said yes to that one.

Cleo ran her finger over the butterfly's bumpy outline. She touched the matching butterfly Passion Clip that Caylee had made special for this occasion, just to make sure it was still in place. The rhinestones on the barrette's wings reflected the sun in dancing dots of light on the minivan's ceiling. Cleo moved her head to make them dance faster.

Her hair was in a fresh twist-n-curl, which Miss Merlean had done for her the night before at Salon Go Natural. Mom had sat in the chair next to Cleo, getting her hair cut in a new, much more chic style. It was a definite improvement.

Cleo had spent almost an hour in the bathroom that morning, mostly working on her hair, but also staring into the mirror, hoping that what she saw there would be okay. "Are we almost there?" she asked, looking out at apartment rooftops, convenience marts, and palm trees, as their minivan zipped through the busy city.

"Where are we going, anyway?" Josh asked. He ran his hands down the sides of his Dodgers cap, cementing it to his freshly shaved head.

"We're going to meet Cleo's birth father, and you and Jay are going to be on your best behavior, remember?"

"We're getting ice cream!" Jay yelled.

"If you show us your *best behavior,*" Mom repeated.

Jay started to sing "The Itsy-Bitsy Spider." It made Cleo feel a little braver, remembering she was like that spider that kept climbing and never gave up.

"So, when are we going to be there?" Cleo rotated her wrist, listening for the click in her joint and to keep from biting her nails, which Mom had polished a glittery lavender color. Normally, Mom wasn't big on Cleo wearing polish. "Beauty comes from the inside," she would preach—plus they chipped quickly and looked horrible, and Cleo didn't take the time to remove the polish properly.

"GPS says ten minutes," Mom said.

Ten minutes. After ten *years* of not knowing anything—or very little, anyway. It was almost too much for her to take.

"How are you doing back there?" Mom asked.

"My insides feel like they're in a blender, my armpits are dripping worse than our bathroom ceiling, and I have to swallow to keep myself from throwing up. But other than that, I'm fine."

Her parents laughed, which helped her to laugh too. She ran her clammy palms over her skirt. She couldn't let him see her sweat. It was a business maxim that went back probably to the days of the ancient Egyptians . . . who, by the way, were ruled by a fierce woman, brave and strong. Cleopatra.

She was Cleopatra! Skimming down the Nile with her entourage, people dedicated to guarding her with their very lives.

Cleopatra the pharaoh commanded loyalty, respect, allegiance. People loved her because they had to!

He would love her.

He had to.

When they pulled into the lot of the Caribbean Café, Cleo thought she might be sick. She was thoroughly nauseated (sitting all the way in the back of the van hadn't helped), and she was pretty sure she'd lost the ability to move her legs.

Her brothers leaped from the van as soon as Mom opened their door. Mom ran after them, yelling something about being in a parking lot.

Cleo stayed put. Her ears buzzed and it was hard to focus. Was she losing her hearing and sight, as well as control of her legs?

Dad's head appeared through the side opening. He grinned. "Ready, Sunshine?"

Cleo focused on his bright smile. Dad had a great smile. Just like her. "I don't think I can do it, Dad."

He paused. His mouth slid to one side and he nodded a bit. "This is a big moment, isn't it? Not too big for us though. We're in this together."

She forced herself to take a deep breath. "Okay. But I mean I literally don't think I can do it. I don't know if I can walk." She bit her lip. "I'm scared, Dad."

He reached out his hand. She grabbed it and took a few wobbly steps to the edge of the opening. She jumped and Dad held on.

They walked toward the café together, Cleo still holding her dad's hand. An open patio seating area was off to the left of the entrance. Mom was already there, talking to a man . . . a black man, with long Afro spikes that sort of burst from his head and hung down almost to his shoulders and he was tall and looked strong and he had intense-looking eyes and he moved his hands a lot when he talked and he wore silver rings and a gold bracelet that flashed and he was looking at Cleo and his smile was huge.

Just like hers.

He reached out his hand.

She hesitated.

"You must be Cleopatra."

She nodded. *Be professional, be professional.* She took his hand and gave it a firm shake. An elaborate tattoo covered his upper right arm, disappearing beneath his shirt. "Hello, Mr. Banks." Her voice had come out more quietly than she intended. She cleared her throat and tried again, looking him in the eye. "Yes. I'm Cleopatra Edison Oliver."

His eyebrows jumped. Smile wrinkles appeared around his eyes. "It's very good to meet you, Cleopatra Edison Oliver."

Cleo tried fried plantains for the first time that day. They were now officially her favorite food. The meal was over but the conversation, which had been nonstop, continued. Cleo, sitting in a booth just a few feet from her birth dad, had done a lot of the talking. About their neighborhood, and their church, and her school, and how much she liked her class and Mr. Boring (his name made Kelvin Banks laugh). And how her best friend lived three houses away in a splendarvelous pink villa, and how she and Caylee had met in second grade and been best buddies ever since and now they were business partners too. She told him about all her businesses so far, but especially her latest, and how they had come up with the name for their personalized barrettes, and their slogan: "Tell the world who you are!" They had sold one hundred and sixty-seven individual Passion Clips already, even to someone as far away as Tokyo, Japan, through Artsy! And they had gotten over a thousand views on FortuneTube and she was expecting to hear from Fortune very soon.

Kelvin Banks had been to the adoption agency and read all the update letters and school pictures Mom had sent over the years, which made Mom gasp and start to cry. Thankfully, she pulled herself together quickly. Cleo didn't want this thing to turn into a big blubberfest.

He asked Cleo about playing basketball—he had played in high school and still played for fun—and told her his favorite team was the LA Lakers, but he would start following the Sparks too, now that he knew it was Cleo's favorite.

She had wanted very badly to ask him about her birth mom, but she didn't want to put him on the spot. Even more, she didn't want to hear something that would dash her hopes that her birth mom was someone super successful, maybe even famous, like Fortune. For now, meeting her birth dad was enough.

She learned that Kelvin Banks was twenty-nine years old, he did arts programming for a Boys & Girls Club, and he loved working with kids and teaching them about expressing themselves through poetry and spoken word and music—all things that he liked to do. She learned that he had recently started playing steel drums.

"I love steel drums!" she exclaimed, which made her parents look at her curiously.

"You do?" Mom said.

"Yeah! Remember, you took me to that Jamaican steel drum concert at the Hollywood Bowl when I was eight?"

"Of course."

"I've loved them ever since!"

"Oh, I didn't realize. That's great."

Kelvin Banks nodded and smiled like he thought it was great too.

"I just had a fantastic idea!" Cleo burst out.

Dad interjected, "If you haven't figured it out already, Cleo is full of fantastic ideas."

Kelvin Banks raised his chin and eyebrows at the same time. "Yes, I was starting to pick up on that."

"Yep." Cleo bobbed her head. "And here's my latest: You could teach me how to play steel drums!"

"Me too!" Jay shouted.

"I want to play drums," Josh cried.

Mom quieted them both.

Kelvin Banks laughed his deep, throaty laugh. He gazed at Cleo from his spot on the bench seat they shared. "You're quite the go-getter, aren't you?" He smiled his brilliant smile.

Cleo felt the prick again, this time sharper than ever, as if a giant bee had plunged its stinger straight into her heart. She looked down, quickly, before her eyes could give away the throbbing in her chest. She nodded.

There was an awkward silence. The first of the whole meal.

"I should probably let your family get on with your day," Kelvin Banks said.

Cleo's head snapped up. "You have to go already?"

Kelvin Banks's eyes shifted back and forth between Cleo's parents. He seemed unsure of what to do or say. "Well, I . . ."

Dad spoke up. "I'll go pay the bill and then we can talk about getting together again."

Cleo's shoulders relaxed.

"Sound good?" Dad asked.

Kelvin Banks reached for his wallet. "Sure, but let me —"

"No, sir," Dad said firmly. "We got this. Really. We're just so grateful . . ." His words trailed off.

Kelvin Banks nodded. "Okay. Thanks."

Dad left the table, the boys trailing after to get the mints they had spied on the way in.

Her birth dad's intense eyes fixed on her. "So, Miss Cleopatra Edison Oliver, I have one more question before I go."

Cleo's breath caught in her throat. Her heart *ka-thunked*. She didn't want him to go.

"Who would you tell the world *you* are?"

Words swirled in her mind like *a mini-tornado*. *Dreamer. Ideas person. Businessgirl. Basketball player. Persuader. Pancake lover. Ladder climber. Leader. CEO.*

The silence stretched as she searched for just the right words. Thankfully, the waiter came to refill their waters, giving her a little longer to think.

Was there anything she could say to make him stay forever?

And what about *her* questions? She had so many! Behind those mysterious, dark brown eyes were answers, she was sure of it. At least there would be another time to ask. Dad had said they would get together again. She took a breath.

"I'm a girl with big dreams who won't let anything stop her. I may be young, I may be small, but I'm as *persistent* as the Itsy-Bitsy Spider." She grinned.

Kelvin Banks got a funny look on his face. He glanced away and for a second Cleo was afraid she'd said something wrong. But when he looked back, his eyes were glistening and he said, "That's exactly how I was when I was your age."

Suddenly, she was flinging her arms around his middle and hugging him as hard as she could. His arms hovered above her, then slowly he embraced her, and the smell of spicy food and the taste of sweet plantains and the feeling of her birth dad's arms around her mingled together and became a memory she would never forget—a coin in the piggy bank of her self that she would never, ever spend.

◆ CHAPTER 19 ◆

Persistence Pays

Cleo sat on her dad's lap at the ice-cream shop, hugging Beary and licking her mint-chip cone. She and her brothers wore the yellow Boys & Girls Club T-shirts that Kelvin Banks had brought them. Meeting her birth dad had satisfied one part of her, but it had stirred another part that was hungrier than ever. She felt like Micah Mitchell's bear that had just woken up from *hypernation*. She laughed to herself and squeezed Beary a little harder.

On the way home, Mom remembered that between clothes shopping, getting their hair done, and soccer games, no one had checked the mail the day before. "Will you grab it, Cleo?"

"Sure!" They pulled into the driveway and Cleo ran to the mailbox. She riffled through the stack of mail. Cardstock ads for a Realtor and gutter cleaners, a couple of bills, the small newspaper of weekly coupons, and then . . . *oh*! Could it really be?

Hidden behind the weekly flyer, a large white envelope with FORTUNE ENTERPRISES, INC. in gold lettering in the upper left-hand corner.

"Mom! Dad!" She sprinted back to the driveway behind their house, but everyone was already inside. She dropped the rest of the mail on the patio table and tore open the envelope. Glossy paper peeked out. A photograph! Thankfully, she hadn't ripped it in her fervor to open the envelope. She pulled out the photo and gazed at it in wonder. Fortune smiled at her, her teeth brilliant, straight, beautiful. And across the bottom, in bold black ink that Cleo traced with her finger, Fortune's signature.

She put the picture down and looked in the envelope. A letter.

This was it. Her big break. Her chance to meet Fortune, the woman who inspired her every day to believe in her destiny.

Cleo's eyes gobbled up the words until she got to "Unfortunately . . ."

She stopped. She couldn't read on. But she had to.

"Unfortunately, as much as I would like to, I cannot have every person on my show who writes in with a fabulous idea."

Every ounce of excitement drained from her heart like water through a sieve.

Fortune went on to say she couldn't help Cleo find her birth parents but wished her luck in her search; told her she must have amazing parents to have raised such a confident, articulate businesswoman; and she was *sure* "we will be hearing big things from Cleo Edison Oliver one day."

Cleo felt like Mom's statuette of a mother holding a baby after Josh hit it with his baseball—in pieces on the ground.

Mom came out the back door. "Everything okay out here?" She looked over Cleo's shoulder. "Honey! It's from Fortune! You heard from her!" She sounded surprised that Fortune had actually written back.

"I did." Cleo's voice had no bounce.

She handed over the letter and Mom scanned it. "Oh. I'm sorry, sweetie. I know you were really hoping . . ." Cleo waited for her to say something about Fortune's comments about searching for Cleo's birth parents, but she didn't.

"Hey, what's this about?" Mom pointed to the bottom of the page. She read the P.S. aloud. "'Make sure you watch the show on Monday, October 31. I will have a special surprise. P.P.S. You won't want to miss it!'

"That sounds intriguing," Mom said. "We'll have to watch."

"Yeah, I suppose." Cleo folded the letter and stuffed it back in the envelope. Fortune's "surprise" was probably just another promotional scheme for FortuneTube, like the call for kid entrepreneurs to upload their business-related videos.

She handed the pile of mail, including Fortune's letter, to Mom. She was tempted to leave the photo on the table, but she snatched it and took it to her room. She put it on her desk, then got Dad's camera and printed out the picture he'd taken of her and Kelvin Banks. She taped it on the wall near her pillow so it would be the last thing she saw before going to sleep and the first thing she saw when she woke up.

Cleo told Caylee all about meeting her birth dad while they made Passion Clips after dinner that night. Cleo could make the artist palette, paintbrush, chef's hat and spoon, and any of the simple-shaped clips like balls, pencils, and journals all on her own. She left the more complicated clips and new clip designs to Caylee.

As usual, Caylee was an excellent listener. Cleo couldn't wait to introduce her to Kelvin Banks.

Cleo also showed her the letter from Fortune.

"So we're watching next Monday, right?" Caylee's eyes gleamed with excitement.

Cleo blew out her breath. "I don't know. I . . . It's just — I was so —" Her voice had started to waver. *She was so sure Fortune would be more interested and supportive.* After all, Cleo had been watching her since she was three years old. There was no one in the world who wanted to be like Fortune more than Cleo!

She focused harder on gluing the small pink piece of felt to the end of the pencil she was making. Gloopy's hot glue dripped on her finger. "Ow!" She stuck her finger in her mouth then stalked out of the room to run it in cold water.

When she came back, neither of them brought up Fortune again, which was just fine with Cleo.

Halloween came. Cleo had been planning to dress up as Fortune A. Davies, but after receiving the bad-news letter she'd decided to reuse her Cleopatra costume instead. The bodice was a little tight and they'd thrown away her staff with the ankh after Josh had broken it in a duel with Jay, but the headdress still fit fine.

When Cleo got home that afternoon, the first thing Mom asked about was watching *Fortune*. Cleo just said, "I need to do my homework before trick-or-treating," and headed to her room. She felt Mom's eyes on her as she sulked upstairs, but she didn't turn around and she didn't say any more.

She sat at her desk, trying to ignore Fortune staring at her from her wall, and made herself read her newest book report book. As it neared four o'clock, her stomach grumbled. Well, she would just duck into the kitchen for a snack, and perhaps if Mom had on the TV, she might hear something, but she wouldn't go in the family room. She wouldn't watch.

Mom was in the living room helping Josh and Jay with their costumes. The TV wasn't on.

Oh well. It was for the best. Cleo raided the cabinet for crackers, grabbed a yogurt from the fridge, and headed back to her room for more reading.

Four o'clock came. Then 4:01. 4:02. 4:03. The minutes ticked away on her digital clock. It was impossible to concentrate. Had the surprise happened already? Would she be terribly disappointed that she hadn't seen it? That was silly. How could she be disappointed if she didn't know what it was and probably never would?

The phone rang downstairs. A moment later, Mom shouted, "Cleo, hurry! Quick!"

Cleo jumped from her chair, adrenaline racing through her bloodstream as if a siren had sounded in her room. She bounded down the stairs. Fortune's voice came from the family room. Had she just said the word *clips*?

Cleo rounded the corner and there on the wide-screen TV in all her glowing glory was Fortune — wearing the pyramid Passion Clips in her hair!!!

Mom handed her the phone, mouthing, "Caylee."

Cleo shrieked into the phone, "She's wearing our clips! She's wearing our clips!"

Caylee yelled, "I know! I know!" and Josh and Jay were asking questions and Barkley was barking and Mom said something to her brothers and they both started cheering and jumping up and down and it was so loud Cleo couldn't hear anything Fortune was saying and before she could get everyone to quiet down, it was time for commercials!

"What'd she say? I didn't hear anything she said!" Cleo wailed.

"She told everyone about Passion Clips, Cleo!" Caylee's voice was pitched high with excitement. "And where to order them on Artsy!"

"Ohmygosh! Ohmygosh! We're going to get so many orders!"

"And she said our names, Cleo! She called you the CEO and me the COO!"

"She *what*? She said our *names*?"

Mom's eyes popped wide in surprise.

Cleo couldn't hold it in any longer. She let out a long, loud scream. If the wild parrots had been roosting in the camphor tree over her house, they would have been frightened into flight. Josh and Jay took this opportunity to yell some more, and Barkley bayed at the top of his lungs.

The TV caught Cleo's attention again. A girl that looked a whole lot like Lexie Lewis was on the screen. Wait a minute. It *was* Lexie Lewis! "Look!" she pointed at the TV. "It's Lexie's Sunshine Sparkle flute-fravored beverage commercial!" She laughed, releasing the nervous energy of the last few minutes.

Lexie was great. She was a natural. Cleo would be sure to tell her at school the next day.

After everyone had finally calmed down, Mom told Cleo that she had actually set the recorder to record *Fortune* that day, just in case Cleo changed her mind. A few minutes later, Dad got home, Caylee ran over, and they all sat down and watched the whole thing together.

Cleo watched it two more times after that, so *so* glad that Mom had captured this incredible moment, and knowing that one day soon, she would share it with her birth dad too.

$$$CEO$$$
Cleopatra Edison Oliver, CEO

CLEOPATRA ENTERPRISES, INC.

818 Camphor Street

Altadena Heights, CA 91120

Fortune A. Davies, CEO

Fortune Enterprises, Inc.

150 Madison Avenue

New York, NY 10016

Dear Ms. Fortune A. Davies:

THANK YOU SO MUCH!!! Seeing you on TV wearing the Passion Clips™ we sent you was the highlight of my life so far ☺ ☺ ☺!!!

Since you spotlighted our business on your show, we have received so many orders that we decided to hire an employee! Her name is Lexie Lewis and she used to be my archenemy, but it turns out she's not so bad. She's just been going through a rough time, although she says it's better now that we've become friends. She's also very careful when it comes to cutting and gluing on small parts, and so we gave her the job.

Also, you're not going to believe this, but I found my birth dad! Or he found me. He is very persistent, just like me. He had some things in his life he needed to work out, but he never gave up hope that one day he would meet me and get to know me, and now that's exactly what we are doing. He is more of a poet and a teacher than a businessman, but I am going to help him with that. ☺ That way he can get more of his poems and raps out into the world for others to read and hear. He's got a lot of important things to say. I am very proud of him.

I wish I had a bigger way to say "thank you," but for now, please accept the enclosed samples of my mom's and my latest product (which will be going to market very soon) as a token of my appreciation. I know how much you love your pharaoh hound,

...efully HE will love these
...azing, handcrafted dog treats,
...anine Cookies™—made with extra
... and a lot of love!

Your friend,

Cleopatra Edison Oliver

Cleopatra Edison Oliver, CEO

P.S. I've enclosed a poem I wrote for class.
My birth dad really liked it (maybe I got some
of his poetry genes!). I hope you like it too.

P.P.S. I went as YOU for Halloween this
year! I wore a big button that said
"Delivering Destinies and Financing Futures"
and carried a large book with a cover that
said "Fortune Principles for How to Build
Your Business and Live the Life You
Want." I was a BIG hit at every house!
Thank you again!!!

"Persistent"

By Cleopatra Edison Oliver

I'm persistent as a dripping faucet:

Drip.

Drip.

Drip.

Dripping without stopping till my mom

Flip-flips.

I won't give up. I've got big dreams.

I have a for-sure destiny . . .

At least that's what it seems.

I'm like a dentist with a scaler,

Cleopatra is my name.

I'm a dog who's caught a scent—

hunting fortune and my fame.

I'm a seed in rocky dirt

growing up into a flower.

I'm the Itsy-Bitsy Spider

and I've got Persuasion Power!

Acknowledgments

I'm thankful to the people who make it possible for me to continue doing what I love. To those at Scholastic who work so hard to get stories into the hands of kids, thank you for all that you do. A special thank you to Arthur A. Levine, whose incisive, "no punches pulled" input helped me to find the deeper, more touching story. Also, huge thanks are due to editorial assistant Weslie Turner for her enthusiastic support, affirming feedback, and diligence with the details. Thanks to Rebekah Wallin for overseeing production; Erica Ferguson for her careful reading of the manuscript; Mary Claire Cruz for her attention to the book's design; and Jennifer L. Meyer for her lovely and whimsical illustrations, which add so much to the finished product. Thank you to my agent, Regina Brooks, for always being for me (and Cleo).

Of course my goal is to connect with kids first and foremost. I'm grateful to my third- and fourth-grade focus group, who gave me honest feedback about what was (and was not) working in this story (over plentiful Jelly Bellies, of course): Skye Frazier, Kaya Terada, Lily Hall, Kahea Lum-Lung, Ruby Lopez, Amina Barga-Smith, and Rosa

Saulter-Edwards (honorary second-grade member). Thank you to Angela Tucker, star of the beautiful documentary *Closure*, about her reunion with her birth family and host of The Adopted Life Episodes, for her helpful feedback on this manuscript. Also to Jill Dziko for answering questions regarding adoption processes, and to Johanna Hernandez, teacher extraordinaire, for assistance with fifth-grade classroom and curriculum questions. Written acknowledgment is long overdue to my own fifth-grade teacher, Janet Mansfield, who first encouraged my love of creative writing and planted the seeds of my career by telling me that I was good at it.

To my dear friends, the Arnolds, and my sister, Fina Arnold, thank you for being my inspiration in more ways than one. Finally, love and gratitude to my husband, Matt, for prompting me to renew my resolve and commit to my calling, and to my daughters, Skye and Umbria: May you discover, love, and use your superpowers.

About the Author

Sundee Frazier is the author of *Cleo Edison Oliver, Playground Millionaire*, which received a starred review from *Booklist*. She won the 2008 ALA Coretta Scott King / John Steptoe New Talent Award for her first novel, *Brendan Buckley's Universe and Everything in It*. Frazier graduated from the University of Southern California with a degree in broadcast journalism in 1991 and earned her MFA in Writing for Children from Vermont College in 2004. She currently lives near Seattle with her husband and two daughters.

THIS BOOK was edited by Arthur Levine and designed by Mary Claire Cruz. The text was set in Electra LT, and the display type was set in GFY Christopha. The book was printed and bound at Command Web in Jefferson City, Missouri. Production was supervised by Rebekah Wallin, and manufacturing was supervised by Angelique Browne.